"Oh, God, I've missed you, Emily."

"Shh. Don't talk, Jake. Just hold me. *Hold* me."

They kissed until their lips felt bruised, and then they lay down together, fully clothed, and caressed each other. Simply caressed.

He didn't speak. Didn't dare. Words might shatter the spell.

And this was surely a spell they were under, the same bit of magic that had overtaken them in Mississippi. With the door shut against the world, they might have been in a time before the avalanche, a time when there was no doubt about their future together.

Still silent, they cast their clothes aside and came together with the fury of two storm fronts colliding over the peaks of Everest.

But what about afterward? Would this power turn against him?

Dear Reader,

'Tis the season to ask yourself "What makes Christmas special?" (other than a Silhouette Special Edition novel in your stocking, that is). For Susan Mallery, it's "sharing in established traditions and starting new ones." And what could be more of a tradition than reading Susan's adorable holiday MONTANA MAVERICKS story, *Christmas in Whitehorn!*

Peggy Webb's statement of the season, "The only enduring gift is love" resonates in us all as she produces an enduring gift with *The Smile of an Angel* from her series THE WESTMORELAND DIARIES. Along with love, author Patricia Kay feels that Christmas "is all about joy—the joy of being with family and loved ones." And we are overjoyed to bring you the latest in her CALLAHANS & KIN miniseries, *Just a Small-Town Girl.*

Sylvie Kurtz shows us the "magical quality" of the holidays in *A Little Christmas Magic*, a charming opposites-attract love story. And we are delighted by Patricia McLinn's *My Heart Remembers* from her WYOMING WILDFLOWERS miniseries. For Patricia, "Christmas is family. Revisiting memories, but also focusing on today." Crystal Green echoes this thought. "The word *family* is synonymous with Christmas." So curl up with her latest, *The Pregnant Bride*, from her new miniseries, KANE'S CROSSING!

As you can see, we have many talented writers to celebrate this holiday season in Special Edition.

Happy Holidays!

Karen Taylor Richman
Senior Editor

Please address questions and book requests to:
Silhouette Reader Service
U.S.: 3010 Walden Ave., P.O. Box 1325, Buffalo, NY 14269
Canadian: P.O. Box 609, Fort Erie, Ont. L2A 5X3

The Smile of an Angel

PEGGY WEBB

![Silhouette]

SPECIAL EDITION™

Published by Silhouette Books

America's Publisher of Contemporary Romance

For my magical, marvelous, magnificent Unicorn.

 SILHOUETTE BOOKS

ISBN 0-373-24436-3

THE SMILE OF AN ANGEL

Copyright © 2001 by Peggy Webb

Visit Silhouette at www.eHarlequin.com

Printed in U.S.A.

PEGGY WEBB

and her two chocolate Labs live in a hundred-year-old house not far from the farm where she grew up. "A farm is a wonderful place for dreaming," she says. "I used to sit in the hayloft and dream of being a writer." Now, with two grown children and more than forty-five romance novels to her credit, the former English teacher confesses she's still a hopeless romantic and loves to create the happy endings her readers love so well.

When she isn't writing, she can be found at her piano playing blues and jazz or in one of her gardens planting flowers. A believer in the idea that a person should never stand still, Peggy recently taught herself carpentry.

My dearest Emily,

I know that your heart must be breaking. You worry if I will be strong enough to make it through while your father lies in a coma. You worry about him. Will you ever feel his embrace again? And you worry about Jake, lost atop K2, the second largest mountain in the world. Your heart is feeling empty because the last words the two of you exchanged were far from loving.

You must have faith that love needs no map, no pathway for two hearts to find their way back to each other. When I was a young girl, there were times when I thought that it would be impossible for your father and me to last a lifetime. But love always pushed pride and fear out of the way, somehow bringing us home.

Emily, don't lose hope. I would bet all the roses in my garden that Jake is going to come down from that mountain and head straight for your arms.

With all my hope and love,

Mom

Prologue

From the diary of Anne Beaufort Westmoreland:

May 10, 2001

I have always loved May in Mississippi. And never more than this year. Not because the azaleas are more spectacular than usual and the forsythia is so heavy with blossoms it looks as if the bushes will break in two. Not because I spotted the bluebirds yesterday coming back to nest in the houses Michael built.

It is Michael who makes this May special, my beloved husband who has made all the days of all the seasons of my life a time to remember. Whether he is here at Belle Rose or off trekking through the wilds, my dearest Michael is always with me.

He's on Everest now, the climber's ultimate challenge, the most unforgiving of places, the mountain I fear most.

But he's promised it will be his last climb. After all these years of capturing the world's most forbidding places on film, he's finally coming home, settling in, returning to the antebellum house we bought and restored together just in time for the family reunion. I hope.

All our children will be here, with the possible exception of our oldest. With Hannah nothing is ever certain. Like her father, she has wanderlust in her blood. She's down in the Amazon doing a story on the disappearing rain forest, right in the thick of things, I'm sure, taking risks that nobody else would take in order to get the right interview, the right picture.

She's Michael's child, all right. As is Emily, our youngest, who doesn't have a domestic bone in her body. Why she prefers to live in a cabin in the woods keeping company with as many wild animals as she can rescue is beyond me. I had hoped that she, at least, would inherit a few traits and talents from me. Well, I can't say she didn't try. When she was ten she volunteered to take piano lessons. Just to please me, I later found out. I thought she was doing so great, too. I'll never forget the day Michael called me to come to the door of the study where she was practicing. Naturally I thought he was pleased as punch, considering he's always loved the way I play the piano. But no, he was grinning like a possum eating berries, holding his sides to keep from bursting out laughing. When I peeked through the crack I saw Emily stretched out on the rug reading a book about the mating habits of the wolf while a tape recorder nearby played a simplified version of "Minuet in G." To this good day I don't know who she bribed to record it for her. Probably Jimmy Clark. She could always get him to do anything she wanted. He married that nice girl from Jackson, Glenda Jean Phipps's granddaughter.

Emily never would go out with him, claimed he was boring.

Well, I guess I ought to understand that. Lord knows, if Michael Westmoreland is anything in this world, it's certainly not boring. He marches to the beat of a different drummer. I never understood the meaning of that phrase until I met him. I never understood a lot of things until I met Michael—how two hearts can recognize each other even before you speak, how neither time nor space can separate two lovers when their souls are irrevocably joined, how a simple touch can become the single most important thing you've ever done.

I think it's no accident he's named for a celestial being, for he's certainly my dear sweet angel. And if I sound like an old fool, what do I care? He's the most important person in my life.

Don't get me wrong. I love my children, all of them, but it's Michael who completes me. With him and only him, I am whole.

I can't wait to see him. The way we carry on together you'd think we were sixteen, instead of fifty-six. Thank goodness not one of our children acts embarrassed or shocked, not even Daniel. Someday some lucky girl is going to find out that underneath those staid and steady pastoral robes of his is a man who is pure gold.

Daniel, our middle child, the son I wanted to look exactly like Michael—thick dark hair and dancing green eyes—but who turned out looking just like me. Except tall.

I guess I'm the luckiest woman alive. And even though I've wished through the years that Michael was here with me, instead of in Nepal or Italy or some other far-flung part of the world, I wouldn't trade places with anybody else. I've had the best part of him—his gen-

erous and loving heart—and in spite of the lonely times
when I've reached to the other side of the bed and found
it empty, I still wouldn't change a thing about my life,
for even a small percentage of Michael is better than a
hundred percent of another man.

So I'm sending a prayer winging upward to speed my
beloved's return to me. And a prayer for all my children, that they will someday know the enchantment, the
amazement, the absolute joy of finding their one true
love.

Chapter One

Emily Westmoreland drove with the windows open so that the musk coming off the skunk curled beside her on the front seat would escape. Hopefully. A skunk's noxious fumes are its only defense, and Gwendolyn had not been defumed. Nor would she ever.

Emily lived in a small cabin in the Tallahatchie River Bottom and worked in animal rescue and rehabilitation. Her job was not to domesticate animals, but to help them return to their natural habitat. Gwendolyn was her latest rescue, but so far she'd shown no signs of preparing to return to the wilderness where Emily had found her with her front leg caught in a trap.

In fact, just the opposite was true. She acted as if she were preparing to move in permanently with Emily, stripes, tail, malodorous fumes and all. And although she only sprayed when she was scared, she was never free of the musky scent.

The sign to Vicksburg came up, and as Emily turned on her blinker, Gwendolyn sat up and peered out the window. Just like a child.

That was how Emily always felt coming home. As full of anticipation as a kid at Christmas. It was more than the prospect of seeing her parents that made her heart beat fast: it was the city itself. Vicksburg, the red-carpet city of the South.

With her windows down Emily could smell the rich black earth, the fecund fragrance that rose up from a place fed by two mighty rivers, the Mississippi and the Yazoo. She could hear the echoes of long-ago battle cries as the Confederates held the bluffs until starvation forced them to surrender. She could hear the soft susurration of wind through the 880 regimental markers that presided over the graves, now grass-covered, of more than twenty thousand Union and Confederate soldiers.

She could see the influence of the Spanish and the French in the little shops and houses that dotted her hometown, a riverport city founded in 1812 on the plantation of William Vick and John Lane. It was a town with such stiff-necked pride in its Southern heritage it didn't celebrate the Fourth of July until late in the twentieth century.

Just ahead stood her parents' house, a glorious 1840s Greek Revival mansion with a union cannonball still lodged in the parlor wall. Though the house had its original gas-lit chandeliers and many of its original antique furnishings, Anne Beaufort Westmoreland had made it a home. She'd put cozy touches throughout and plenty of rocking chairs on the verandahs so that you could sit in comfort while you listened to the music of two rivers converging.

Emily stopped just inside the gates to gaze at the rivers and breathe the greening air of spring. It wrapped its arms around her like a warm blanket, dear, familiar and comforting. And though she'd lived in a small log cabin for the past seven years, this was the place she called home.

"We're almost there. Now listen, Gwendolyn. Mother and Daddy are going to love you. Still, this is new territory. You stick by me. Understand?"

Emily felt better for having given instructions. Not that the skunk understood. Or even needed them. She followed Emily everywhere. If she walked in figure eights, so did Gwendolyn. If she zigzagged, so did Gwendolyn.

And when Emily put her in her cage, Gwendolyn cried. That was why Emily had ended up going to her family's reunion with a skunk in tow.

There really wasn't any reason for her to worry, though. She'd brought home wild animals even as a child. Her parents wouldn't be surprised by one little skunk.

She'd have a lovely visit with them, and after all the Westmoreland kin arrived, she'd stick around just long enough to say hi to the aunts and uncles and cousins with their husbands and all their babies, then head back to the deep woods.

Not that she had anything against husbands and children, or even love, for that matter. Lord knows, her parents set such an example that Emily was absolutely certain love existed. It just wasn't for her, that was all. It didn't fit her lifestyle.

She was a free spirit, and that was the way she planned to stay. No encumbrances. No messy emotions. No entanglements.

One last look at the water, one quiet, meditative moment, and Emily drove up the winding drive to Belle Rose, where her parents waited. Following the sound of laughter and music, she found them beside the gazebo in the garden behind the house, her father looking rugged and handsome, and her mother looking as if she'd been given the moon.

"Mom! Dad!" Emily was racing toward them with Gwendolyn hard on her heels when the most outrageously gorgeous man she'd ever seen stepped out of the gazebo.

All of a sudden she took back everything she'd ever said or thought about freedom and independence and living all by herself in the deep woods.

The man was a complete stranger to her, and yet her heart recognized him, knew him as intimately as if they'd spent the past hundred years together.

Riveted, her breath caught in her throat, her heart beating double time, Emily smiled. It was a good beginning, wasn't it?

Her father held out his arms. "Emily, come over here. I want you to meet Jake Bean."

His name flowed through her like a river, like a poem, like a song. And so, smelling suspiciously of skunk, Emily walked toward the gazebo to meet the man who had just turned her world upside down.

Jake had known that Michael Westmoreland had two daughters. What he hadn't known was that the youngest would pack such a punch. She was enchanting, a dark-haired sprite with the smile of an angel and the wicked gleam of a mischief-maker in her green eyes. Altogether charming and totally off-limits.

Not only because she was Michael's daughter, but because she set Jake's blood astir. He wasn't about to allow any woman to do that to him. First the libido got out of hand, then the heart, and the next thing you knew you were waltzing down the aisle with a woman who cried every time you packed your gear and headed to the mountains. A woman who didn't understand why you'd want to leave her all alone while you risked your life challenging the highest peaks.

Besides that, he was a man whose life depended on getting the details right. He'd read every book and knew every rule about mountain climbing. But he'd never seen a manual about romance, and he was far too intelligent to embark on an adventure that had no rules.

And so he returned her smile. Anything less would have been impolite, wouldn't it?

"My goodness," she said, sounding suddenly out of breath. "Daddy's just like me. Always bringing somebody home." She held out a small hand that got lost in his. "Hello, Jake. I'm Emily, the family's answer to Marlin Perkins."

That was when he saw the skunk behind her. Smelled it, too. Both the exotic creatures standing in front of him gave off a slightly musky scent that wasn't altogether unpleasant.

He'd say one thing for Michael's daughter: she certainly was different from most of the women he met. They wore fragrances like Chanel No. 5 and wouldn't dream of keeping company with a skunk, much less bringing one to a family reunion.

"Hello, Emily." Lord, she had the prettiest eyes he'd ever seen. He couldn't seem to look away from them. "I hope you don't mind my intrusion into this family affair."

"Not at all. There's always been enough love in this family to go around...and the food, goodness, you should see the food that's brought in for our family reunions. Well, of course, you *will* see it."

Jake was fascinated and pleased. He didn't know there were any women left in this world who blushed, and he certainly didn't know any who got flustered in his presence. Lord knows, he wasn't much to look at. Windburned, weatherbeaten and lanky. That about summed him up.

While Emily was...well, it would take him a day or two to think of all the adjectives to describe her. Pretty. Soft and sweet. She was also strong and independent. He would have known that about her even if she hadn't brought a skunk to the family mansion.

"Michael told me that your aunt Janice makes the best fried chicken this side of the Mississippi. I guess that's why I tagged along."

Liar. He'd accepted Michael Westmoreland's invitation because he couldn't face the prospect of going back to Atlanta to an empty apartment and a group of friends who acted as if mountain climbing were a disease he'd get over.

So did his mother, in spite of the fact that Jake's father had been one of the world's great climbers. Her dire prediction, which she issued with depressing regularity, was this: you're going to fall and kill yourself, just like your father.

In mountaineering there are two kinds of falls, the unexpected kind where suddenly you're five feet off the wall and descending at a constant acceleration of thirty-two feet per second, where you don't have time to think, where you're plummeting downward still frozen in climbing position.

Then there's the second kind where you've misjudged your strength, your stamina, and you know that you'll never make the next step. There's the slow buildup of tension where you have time for remorse and the painful knowledge that within the next few seconds you could die.

The first kind of fall. That was what was happening to him now. The unexpected kind. The freefall.

Jake still had this mental image of himself as a solo climber, going ever upward, but in fact, he was rapidly descending into a pair of wide green eyes. He wondered if the impact would destroy him.

Here lies Jake Bean, formerly wild and free, now totally domesticated.

To top it all off, he realized he was still holding Emily's hand. He let it loose, then he started casting about for something to discuss besides fried chicken or the weather.

That was when Michael rescued him.

"Nonsense. You didn't tag along. I twisted your arm. I wanted my family to meet the world's greatest climber while I'm still breathing that rarified air."

"This latest expedition was Michael's last climb."

Michael's beautiful wife slid her arm around her husband's waist and gazed at him with such love shining in her eyes Jake had to look away.

Could it be possible to have it all, the passion for the unforgiving places and the love of a good woman? Was it possible that Jake had been wrong all these years?

Here was Emily, smiling up at him, invitation clearly written in her eyes, and he saw how it might be possible to win her. The trick, though, would be to keep her.

How had Michael done it? How had he managed to spend half his time away from home and still keep a woman like Anne Beaufort Westmoreland not only satisfied, but radiantly happy?

Jake wasn't fixing to find out. He wasn't fixing to mess up a good, satisfying life by bringing a woman into the mix, certainly not Michael's daughter. Jake had too much respect for the man to tamper with the affections of his daughter.

"Anne just wants me home so I can cook," Michael said.

"Precisely, darling. Don't you think it's about time to fire up the grill?"

Here was Jake's chance to escape. Here was his chance to restore his sanity.

"I'll help. I know my way around a grill better than I know my way around a mountain."

"Don't believe a word of it," Michael warned the women. "This man thrives on thin air."

Anne laughed. "If you think I'm letting Michael get out of my sight for one minute..." With her cheeks flushed, she looked almost as young as her daughter. "You two stay here and get acquainted, while Michael and I heat things up."

"We might even get around to the grill." Michael swung his wife off her feet, then raced to the house with her, laughing.

There was no escape for Jake now.

Jake looked as uncomfortable as she felt. For the first time since she could remember, Emily was miffed about her parents' obsession with each other. What could they have been thinking, going off and leaving her with a man who obviously wished she would climb into a hole and pull the dirt in after her?

Certainly they weren't matchmaking. That wasn't their style. They didn't believe in contrived relationships; they believed in true love, the kind that reached up and hit you over the head with a two-by-four. The kind that had whacked her between the eyes when she first saw Jake.

A lot of good it did her.

Well, she'd never been one to cry over what might have been. Face the music. That was her style.

"Look, Jake, let's get a few things out in the open. You're obviously not bowled over by my company, and that's fine with me. But you're a guest in my home, and I'm duty bound to play the Southern hostess. So we might as well make the best of it."

"Don't feel duty bound on my account. I can fend for myself."

"Believe me, if we were at my cabin in the woods, I'd

let you. But here at Belle Rose we mind our manners. Otherwise, it's off to the woodshed.''

That coaxed a smile. "I can't imagine either Michael or Anne wielding that much authority.''

"They don't. They let us all run wild. It was Grandma Beaufort who taught us manners.'' She laughed. "Or tried to.''

"Will I get to meet her?''

"Oh, yes. She'll be here with bells on. Literally. She carries a little teatime bell around in her purse, and when she wants something from somebody, she rings the devil out of it.''

Now that he had smiled, Emily was feeling much more comfortable with him.

"Do you mind if I kick off my shoes?'' she asked.

"Be my guest.''

"Grandma Beaufort would be horrified.''

"I promise not to tell.''

Jake's smile got wider. Maybe that was the secret to all this relationship business. Just forget about impressing somebody and be yourself.

"It was a long drive and my feet got hot. Besides, I do love the feel of fresh spring grass on my bare feet.'' She sank her feet into the grass. "Ah, that feels so good.''

"You make it sound that way.''

"Join in if you want. Nobody's here except you and me and Gwendolyn. She won't tell, and I can keep a secret, too.''

"I'll pass for now.''

He sat down in a wrought-iron chair and stretched his long legs. Emily felt like drooling. Instead, she wiggled her toes.

"What made you choose to live in the woods with animals, Emily?''

"I like the ones in the woods better than the ones in the cities."

He threw back his head and roared. It was a beautiful sound, and all of a sudden Emily realized how quiet her cabin was and how she missed the sound of a man's laughter. It was a sound that had punctuated her childhood, her father laughing and tossing one of them in the air, the children or their mother, whoever was handy.

Emily knew their wonderful marriage was rare, and she wondered if she'd ever have anything that even approached it. Maybe that was one of the reasons she'd decided she was better off by herself. Better to be independent and sometimes lonely but usually content than to be married and to know you'd settled for less.

"Is your sister like you?"

"Worse. The animals I rescue in the woods of northeast Mississippi are tame compared to the exotic ones she encounters. She's a photojournalist."

"Yes, your father told me. And your brother's a preacher."

"Yes. Methodist. I'm glad you used that good old Southern term. Your accent doesn't suggest you're Southern. Are you?"

"Not by birth. I was born in Colorado. After my father died, my mother moved us to Atlanta to be close to her people. I was fourteen."

"Was he a climber, too? Don't answer that if you don't want to. I'm nosy."

"What you are is a fresh breeze." Emily was as pleased as if he'd handed her a bouquet of hothouse roses. "You speak your mind, don't you."

"Yes. I guess it comes from living by myself."

"It comes from Michael. You're very much like your father."

Obviously Jake meant that as a compliment, too. For hadn't he come home with Michael?

"That's what everybody says."

"To answer your question, yes, my dad was a climber. He died trying to rescue a party stranded on McKinley during a snowstorm."

"I'm sorry."

She thought how often her own father had been in precarious situations, how she and her mother and her siblings would gather around the television alternating between listening to the weather channel and Tom Brokaw's commentary of rescue efforts taking place on the very mountain where Michael Westmoreland was filming. How they'd all live this sort of half-life until the telephone rang to tell them Michael was safe at base camp, that he'd never gone to the higher elevations, that he'd heeded early-warning signs of bad weather.

Now they would never have to worry about that again.

"It's a risk all climbers take," Jake said.

"Did you ever think about not taking the risks?"

"No. Did you ever think about doing anything besides what you do?"

"Not for one minute. And I would spit in the eye of anybody who tried to dissuade me."

"I'll be careful of my eyes around you, Miss Emily."

He was playing with her, teasing her, and darned if she didn't like it. Too much. Face it, a man as good-looking as Jake was bound to know his way around women. So he'd sized her up right away and seen that it wouldn't take much to charm her, a woman who spent most of her life in the woods and didn't give a flitter for social graces.

He was laying it on thick. For what purpose, she couldn't imagine. First he'd acted as if he couldn't wait to escape to a hot grill, and now he was actually relaxed and smiling and apparently having a good time.

She was too practical to believe the change had a thing to do with her. True, she had good hair and eyes, thanks to her father, but she had absolutely none of her mother's easy charm and grace. Not one iota.

In high school and college she'd had her share of dates, but she'd always been just "one of the boys." That was what they used to tell her. "Emily, you're so much fun to be around you're just like one of the boys."

Sitting in the presence of the world's most desirable man, she lost both her breath and her good sense. He'd made a nice riposte, and she couldn't think of a single thing to say that would be even remotely construed as smart or witty or charming.

She wished she'd paid more attention to Grandmother Beaufort's favorite lecture: how a Southern woman wins her man. She and Hannah used to make faces at each other behind their grandmother's back while she was droning on and on, warming to her subject.

"Now, girls," she'd say. "Listen to me. I ought to know. I've been married five times. Outlived every one of them." The last one had been poor Jackson Perkins, who had let Elizabeth Beaufort lead him around by the nose. After she buried him, she went back to using her first husband's name, claiming he was the only one she'd ever truly loved.

Rule number one. Emily could almost hear her grandmother's intonation. *Let the man chase you till you catch him.*

Now what the devil did that mean?

"Emily?" She looked at Jake like somebody coming out of a dream. Or a nightmare: Woman Smelling of Skunk

Meets World's Sexiest Man. "Did I say something to offend you?"

"Offend me? No, of course not. My mind just wandered off, that's all."

"Happens to me all the time. It comes from living by yourself."

Well, she was fixing to put a big A-plus by his name. She'd always believed the mark of a truly good man was one who never, *ever,* under any circumstances whatsoever made you feel bad about yourself. If, in addition, he turned an awkward situation to your advantage so you also felt validated and even complimented, he joined the ranks of *hero.*

"Thank you, Jake."

"You're welcome."

She loved it that he understood why she was thanking him, loved it that he didn't pretend false modesty. She despised posing and posturing.

To show Jake how much she appreciated him, she sat there with her toes curled into the grass and smiling. She hoped he wouldn't think her idiotic. She hoped he wouldn't think her flirtatious and silly.

Goodness gracious, if she had to win a man acting silly, she'd just go on being content all by herself.

"Emily. Jake." It was her father, calling from the back veranda. "Dinner will be ready in ten minutes."

When she first drove up she'd been starved, ready to eat an elephant. But that had been an hour ago. Before she met Jake.

Before she met the other half of her soul.

"Shall we?" Jake offered his arm, and Emily walked off feeling like a queen. Even after she discovered she'd forgotten her shoes.

* * *

One of the things Emily loved most about coming back to Belle Rose was the late-night chats she had with her mother. She'd missed that.

"Mom?"

Her mother was curled up on a plush velvet love seat, pink satin robe tucked around her feet, open diary in her lap.

"Come in, darling. I've been expecting you."

"You have? I mean, with Dad home and all...I don't want to keep you."

"He's not as young as he used to be. Let's give him a little rest."

She patted the cushion, and Emily sat down beside her.

"You two are perfectly outrageous, did you know that?"

"Yes. Isn't it wonderful?"

"I've always thought so...and pitied the kids whose parents didn't act like you and Dad." Anne reached for her hair, and Emily leaned closer for her mother's strokes. "How did it happen? How did you know to pick him and not somebody else?"

"I *knew*. If it's true love, you always know."

Her mother's reply thrilled Emily all the way to the bone. Could it be true? Could the heart-leaping recognition she'd experienced this afternoon mean what she hoped?

All through dinner, she'd questioned her judgment, second-guessed herself, rationalized. There she'd been with Gwendolyn curled at her feet while Jake practically ignored her. To be fair, he hadn't really ignored her; he'd merely engrossed himself in conversation with her parents.

Occasionally he'd look her way, his eyes burning briefly into hers, then he'd turn his attention back to them. Of course, that was the polite thing to do. After all, he was *their* guest. Not hers.

"This is about you and Jake, isn't it."

"Yes." There was no use playing coy with her mother. She never had and she didn't intend to start. "How did you know?"

"Your Dad and I both saw it. We're thrilled, by the way."

"You're putting the horse before the cart. I don't think Jake's quite as taken with me as I am with him. In fact, I don't think he even likes me very much. I'm not exactly date bait."

"Do you want to be?"

"I'd rather be covered with peanut butter and hung out for the birds, Grandmother Beaufort's advice, notwithstanding."

The two of them were laughing heartily when Michael came through the door, grinning.

"What's going on in here? Girl stuff? Or can I join in?"

"Are you bearing food?" Anne asked.

"Voilà." He produced a big bowl of popcorn from behind his back. "With butter."

"Then hurry." Anne scrunched toward the middle of the love seat to make room for Michael on her other side.

"Where's Jake?" he asked. "Maybe we ought to ask him to join us."

Emily could picture it. Michael's booming cordiality. Jake's feeling obligated. Her feeling uncomfortable. Like somebody's ugly stepdaughter who had to be pawned off on an unsuspecting stranger.

"I think he's already gone to bed. And I don't think that's a very good idea, anyhow."

Her father scrutinized her in that way he always did when he was reading his children's minds. Hannah called him a guru, Emily called him psychic and Daniel called him intuitive. But whatever it was, not one of his children ever tried to fool their father.

The great thing about him was this: although he had the insight of the wizard Merlin, he believed in letting them make their own choices, learn from their own mistakes and grow from their own triumphs while he stood by offering guidance, love and strong arms to catch them if they fell.

"Have some popcorn." He passed Emily the bowl and gave her another of his deep scrutinies. "He's a very fine man, Emily. Solid as a mountain."

"Thank you, Daddy." She stood up and kissed both her parents. "I think I'll turn in."

"Good night," they said, and when she left them, they were sitting close together with their hands in the popcorn bowl. It made Emily happy and lonely at the same time.

As soon as she got back to her room she'd talk to Gwendolyn about that.

Chapter Two

May 11, 2001

There are certain moments I wish I could pluck like a rose and press between the pages of a book. Today was one of them. First there was Michael. I was sitting in the swing reading and suddenly there he was, standing on the front porch smiling at me. "Good morning," he said, as if he'd just walked out of the bedroom we've shared for thirty-five years, instead of off a mountaintop on another continent. We kissed as if he'd been off at war for four years, instead of off filming for four months.

This is the miracle of Michael and me. Our love is as fresh and exciting as the day we met. Lord, I'll never forget that day. It was in New Jersey at the bus station. Both of us headed to New York, I to my classes at Juilliard, Michael to a meeting with elite mountaineer and acclaimed filmmaker Lanford Hayes. I was sitting beside the only window in the bus station, reading a book, not engrossed but interested. Something made me look up, and there he was, the love of my life, a tall, dark-haired man with the most marvelous cheekbones I'd ever seen, a really good-looking stranger who didn't feel like a stranger at all, but somebody I'd known for years. Known and loved.

I looked at him and smiled. That was what brought him to me, he later said. That smile. Brought him past all those empty seats straight to the corner where I sat in the sunshine reading a book.

We started a conversation and couldn't quit. Didn't want to quit. The beautiful thing is that our conversation is still going on after all these years. Michael is like a magnificent eagle. Everything about him soars—his mind, his spirit, his soul, his heart.

From the moment we saw each other, we knew. We knew we were meant to be together, that we'd been together through the millenniums, that we'd always be together. Though we were strangers, our hearts recognized each other.

A love like that is so rare, so perfect, so beautiful, that to deny it is sacrilege.

I saw that recognition again today. In Emily and Jake. Michael did, too. That's why we went off like a couple of teenagers intent on necking. Which we did. And I have the beard burn to prove it.

"Nothing would make me happier," Michael told me about Emily and Jake. "He's as fine a young man as I've ever known."

"I hope they're like us, Michael." That's what I said,

and that's what I meant, but when he pulled me close and kissed my hair and whispered, "No one could ever be like us," I felt as if I owned the world.

And I do. Oh, I do.

Chapter Three

Jake was sitting at the window reading a book and occasionally looking out at the moon and longing—for what, he didn't know—when all of a sudden his door began to ease open. Riveted, his heart beating double time, he watched it open bit by bit.

Could it be…?

"Emily?"

The crack got wider and in walked Gwendolyn. She trotted straight to his chair, then curled up on top of his feet. And he'd swear she was smirking.

Now what? He didn't dare pick her up for fear of making her mad. They'd never get the odor out of the house if she sprayed.

Then there was another consideration: he couldn't take her back to her rightful owner for fear of what he would do. He couldn't be alone with Emily in her bedroom. There was only so much temptation a man could bear.

What to do?

While he was pondering the question, he heard footsteps in the hall, followed by a soft voice.

"Gwendolyn? Gwendolyn? Where are you?"

"In here," Jake said, then waited. It had been three hours since he'd seen her at dinner. Had time restored his sanity? When she walked through his door, would she be just another pretty woman?

The door swung wide, and there she was, framed in his doorway. Jake went into free fall.

"Jake? My goodness, how in the world did she get in here?"

"The door was cracked open."

"I see."

Emily hovered around the doorway as if it offered some kind of safety. And Jake guessed it did. If what he was feeling showed on his face, she must be mortified.

Or maybe not. What if she felt the same thing? What if she wanted to touch him as much as he wanted to touch her? That would rank right up there with one of the seven wonders of the world, but what if it was true? And what if Jake sat there in his chair like a dolt and let the best thing that had ever happened to him pass him by?

That was how he was thinking of her now. The best thing that had ever happened to him. A small miracle. A bit of magic.

"I would have brought her to you, but I thought she might spray if I tried to move her."

A partial truth. From Jake who prided himself on honesty. It would have to do.

"No. She only sprays when she's frightened, and obviously she's not scared of you. In fact, it looks as if she's fallen in love."

Her choice of words delighted him, and so did the blush

that crept into her face the minute they were out of her mouth.

"I've never had anybody in love with me. Skunk or otherwise."

"Oh, my."

Such a soft feminine sound, that sigh she made. It went straight to Jake's heart. Straight to his bones, particularly his backbone, and so he did what any red-blooded male would do when faced with the female of his choice.

He eased the sleeping Gwendolyn aside, then strode across the room, drew Emily inside and shut the door.

She looked at him with shining eyes, and he kissed her. Such a kiss. One that stole his breath, heated his blood and turned all his carefully held convictions upside down.

She was soft and feminine, as he knew she would be. Sweet and hot at the same time. A heady combination of innocence and eroticism. A once-in-a-lifetime woman.

Jake read a lot, enjoyed movies and great blues, but he'd never been one for Broadway tunes. And yet, as he kissed her, one popped into his head. He couldn't even remember where he'd heard it. Recently, it seemed. Probably on Michael's radio. He was always working to the sound of music. Any kind. It didn't matter to him.

"It Only Takes a Moment." That was what hummed through Jake's head. Through his blood.

He embraced this new feeling. Reveled in it.

He pulled her closer, deepening the kiss, and her response stole his breath. Coming up for air, she leaned back in his arms and whispered, "Wow!"

That's exactly what he'd been thinking, and so he kissed her again. It was the headiest experience of his life, Mount Everest included.

But how could that be? How could a sane, sensible man who only a few hours earlier had declared to himself all the reasons he wouldn't get involved with Emily West-moreland all of a sudden find himself involved up to his eyebrows?

Her lips still on his, her delicious body curved intimately into him, she made soft murmuring sounds that drove reason from his mind. Magic, that was what it was. Pure, unadulterated magic. The kind he hadn't felt since he was ten years old and imagined himself standing on top of the highest mountain in the world.

They were two comets colliding.

What had started as a touch of the lips had turned into an explosion of passion that threatened to set the curtains on fire. They weren't kissing; they were making love with their clothes on.

The bed was so close all Jake had to do was back her up a few steps, then lower her to the covers. It was what both of them wanted. More than wanted. What both of them craved.

And yet, he was in her father's house. Practically a stranger to Emily. And she to him. He didn't know whether she was a night owl or a morning person. He didn't know whether she liked to get up early and watch the sunrise or curl back under the covers and get an extra forty winks. He didn't know if she took cream and sugar in her coffee or nothing at all. He didn't even know if she *liked* coffee. Or movies. Or books. Or blues played by James Cotton and his soulful harmonica.

And he didn't care. All he cared about was the incredible magic that had overtaken him.

"I guess we know where this is leading," he said.

"Mmm. Yes, I know."

She rubbed her cheek against his chest. Kittenlike. Adorable. Sexy. Jake had to rein in the wild beast inside of him.

"Not here, though," he said.

"No, not here."

"Atlanta, then. My place. I have some time before I go on another climb."

"No. Mine. I can't get somebody on this short notice to do my job. But be forewarned. My place is only a cabin in the woods."

"I'll follow you home." He kissed her again. "I'll follow you anywhere."

"Mmm. I like the sound of that."

He wrapped her close and kissed her as if he'd been her lover for years, as familiar with her body as his own. And that was how it felt. As if they'd known each other always. Intimately.

"You make it very hard to resist that bed," he said.

"So do you."

"I suppose it would look funny if we left for the woods in the middle of the night."

"Grandmother Beaufort would definitely not approve."

"How about Michael and your mother?"

"They'd not only approve, they would give their blessing. In fact, they already have."

Had he been so easy to read? He thought he'd been so clever at concealment. All through dinner he'd made conversation with the senior Westmorelands when the thing he'd wanted to do was disappear through the French doors with their youngest daughter.

"I was never any good at poker, either," he said.

Emily laughed. "My parents have a special gift for spotting…things like this."

What had she been about to say? In fact, what was there to say about the two of them? Were they merely two people who brought out the lust in each other?

He wasn't about to analyze it. Analysis might be the stuff of reason, but it was the death of miracles. He'd learned that the hard way on the face of a mountain. In the midst of a snowstorm. Lost. With nothing but instinct to guide him home.

Where were his instincts leading him now?

Emily was lolling in Jake's arms—in his *bedroom,* for goodness sake—as if she were some kind of siren who drew men by the score. And it felt so good!

How it had happened was a mystery to her, but she wasn't about to question her good fortune.

That was the way she was thinking now. That Jake was her gift from the universe. Somebody designed especially for her, then set in her path so she couldn't miss him. Not even if she'd tried.

Practical to the bone, she would never have considered such an idea, much less embraced it as her own if it weren't for her parents. They were living proof that such things did happen: that romance could pop up in the most unexpected places, that it could grab you by the heart and not let go, and that it could be not only the most magical thing to ever happen to you but the most endurable.

Somewhere in the far reaches of the house the grandfather clock chimed twelve.

"The witching hour," she said.

"You've bewitched me."

Maybe Jake said that to all the women, but Lord! it felt as if he'd never said it to anyone except her.

"I suppose I should go back to my room."

"Tell me what your bed is like so I can picture you sleeping there."

"It's an antique, a massive four-poster that sits so high off the floor I either have to use a footstool to climb in or take a flying leap and jump."

"And you usually race across the floor and jump."

"Yes. How did you know?"

"An educated guess. You strike me as somebody who does everything with flair...including making love."

He slid his fingers into her hair and tipped her face upward. She drowned in his eyes, a slow exquisite death. If a simple touch had that much power over her, what would it be like to make love with him?

She intended to find out. And soon.

"We'll leave tomorrow," she whispered. "Right after lunch."

"I hope lunch is at 9:00 a.m." He laughed.

She loved his laugh. It was rich and deep, extraordinarily masculine. She loved the way laugh lines fanned out from his eyes, the way his mouth curved upward and stayed there, as if he were the kind of man who laughed often.

"It's at two. If we're lucky we'll be on the road by three."

"I'll eat fast."

She memorized his face with her fingertips, then traced the beautiful curve of his lips.

"Till tomorrow, Jake."

He kissed her again, just as she'd wanted him to. And oh, it was the kind of kiss that set her heart on fire.

"Till then, Emily."

She was so excited she almost forgot Gwendolyn. And when they got back to her room, she leaned against the door, dreaming with her eyes wide open.

Chapter Four

Emily had always been gifted with the ability to fall asleep no matter where she was or what the circumstances. In spite of the fact that Jake raced through her blood like fire, she slept the sleep of the innocent. At the first crack of light through her window, she flung on her robe and raced outside to watch the sunrise.

Anne was already on the front porch. Smiling, she handed Emily a cup of coffee.

"I knew you'd come. It's about the only trait I passed on to you." Anne turned her face to the rising sun. "Isn't it spectacular?"

"Yes. The sleepyheads don't know what they're missing."

They watched the sun fling ribbons of ever-deepening color across the sky, vermilion and orange and gold. And when it was all over, when the brilliance of the sun had overtaken everything except blue, Emily turned to her

mother with the question that had been burning in her mind
ever since she'd left Jake's bedroom.

"What would you say if I told you that I've invited Jake
home with me?"

"I would say *good*."

One of the wonderful things about her parents was that
neither of them had ever made their children feel foolish
by asking a lot of unnecessary questions. Anne didn't ask
when this happened or how or why. She simply trusted her
daughter. That was one of the reasons Emily felt safe con-
fiding in her.

"You don't think it's too soon? I mean, I hardly know
him. He's practically a stranger to me..."

"And yet you feel as if you've known him forever?"

"That's exactly how I feel. But still...I don't know if
I'm doing the right thing."

"What are your instincts saying?"

"They're saying yes."

"Trust them. It's angels whispering in your ear."

"What if it's just my libido talking? What if I'm making
a mess of things? Wouldn't it be better to get to know him
first, go to the movies and out to dinner, that sort of thing,
before I haul off and invite him into my bed?"

Anne's hearty laughter drew Michael to the porch. He
kissed her softly on the lips, the cheeks and the eyes, then
wrapped his arms around her and winked at his daughter
over his wife's shoulder.

"Good morning, Emily. It's good to hear two of my
favorite girls laughing. Is it a private joke or can I join in?"

"You're a central part of this, my love. I was just getting
ready to show Emily my diary."

"The whole thing?"

"Only part of it. Don't worry, darling. Your secrets are
safe with me."

She went into the house and came back with two pages from her diary, turning a bit yellow with age.

"Here. Read these. I think they'll throw some light on all those questions you have."

"Thanks, Mom." Emily sat on the porch with her parents and finished her coffee, then went back into her bedroom and sat in the chair beside the window to read.

October 13, 1966

I can't believe I'm here at the Algonquin Hotel with an intimate stranger, instead of sitting at a grand piano in Juilliard practicing Beethoven's "Pathetique." I say "intimate" because that's exactly how I've been with Michael, the man I met only this afternoon, the man who is now sleeping on our tumbled bed.

I will sit in the sun, I told myself when I walked into the bus station today, and that's the same thing he told himself.

And now, I think our words were prophetic, referring not merely to a resting place, but to a philosophy of life. For what can be a better description of the magic that happened here in this room than to say, "Yes, we embraced the warmth, the brilliance, the life-giving power of the sun."

I shudder to think of my loss, or our loss, if either of us had hesitated, if we had let reason rule rather than the heart. What we would have missed if we'd ducked behind convention, bowed to propriety, caved in to society's censure!

I know his name, Michael Westmoreland, his home, Alabama, the state next door to my own Mississippi, and his profession, aspiring high-altitude filmmaker. Not much. And certainly not enough to satisfy Mother, who has made a practice of being courted exactly six months before she ever let any of her husbands-to-be kiss her. I think that's rule number nine.

I will deal with her later. What I'm dealing with now—no, reveling in—is a miracle.

And knowing the details of his life is not important. What I know about Michael is this: he has a generous heart, a beautiful soul and a wonderful spirit. That is enough.

The moon has tracked westward, and a patch of moonlight is shining through the window onto his hair. It's the blackest I've ever seen, blacker than a crow's wing, thick and crisp. Right now it seems the whole universe is caught up in his hair, and what I want to do more than anything is run my fingers softly through it until he awakes and looks at me with those deep green eyes.

Then I will drown once more. We will both drown. And be reborn.

Chapter Five

With all her feelings validated by her mother's diary, Emily fed Gwendolyn, then went in search of Jake. She'd been away from him for nine hours, and that was too long. Besides, she wanted to spend some time alone with him before a hoard of relatives arrived.

She found him on the path in the deep woods behind Belle Rose, sighted him through the trees just around the curve. Jake Bean in jogging shorts was enough to make a woman drool, and that was exactly what Emily did. He hadn't seen her yet, so she just stood on the path feasting her eyes on his body, every inch of it gorgeous.

He was the one working out, and yet she was the one who felt as if she'd run the better part of the Boston Marathon.

"Can you believe it, Gwendolyn? That gorgeous hunk is going home with us. How did I get so lucky?"

* * *

Jake heard Emily before he saw her. Heard her and smiled.

He put on a burst of speed, and when he rounded the corner and saw her in the sun filtering through the trees, he thought, This is the way it ought to be. This sizzle of excitement. This heart-in-throat joy. This sense of wonder.

"How did *we* get so lucky?" he said, then closed the distance between them and scooped her into his arms. Her smile dazzled him. He felt ten feet tall because it was for him. Only for him.

"You heard?"

"Yes. The canopy of trees creates an acoustic effect. Voices carry out here."

"I guess I ought to be embarrassed, but I'm not."

"Good. I especially liked the 'gorgeous hunk' part."

"Well, you are. Compared to you, I'm a toad."

"You're the most remarkable woman I've ever known."

Then, to show her he meant what he said, he kissed her, one of those long, lingering kisses that felt as if his soul had just flown out of his body and gone to nestle with hers. To his astonishment he discovered that being close to her gave him the same sense of exhilaration as standing on the highest peak of a mountain.

Other climbers talked about conquering mountains, but he knew better. You could no more conquer a mountain than you could conquer a good woman. Nor should you want to or even try, for to conquer was to take away the very thing you desired. That sense of challenge. Of achievement. Of vaulting freedom.

And most of all, of hope.

Emily was hope wrapped in his arms, and he held on to her, held her with tenderness and passion and awe.

"I wish we could stand in these woods and do this forever,'' she said at last, leaning back and beaming up at him. "But the relatives will be arriving soon."

"I should change, then."

"Not on my account. It's Edna Sue I'm worried about."

"A maiden aunt?"

"No. A man-eating cousin. I don't want her after you."

He chuckled. "Are you trying to protect my reputation?"

"No. My motives are purely selfish. I want to be the only one eyeing your delicious body."

"Delicious?"

"Oh, yes. I can tell by looking. I can't wait to find out if I'm right."

This sort of refreshing honesty was new to Jake. Actually, it was all new to Jake. In his thirty years, he'd had very little time for women. From the time he'd discovered that he wanted to be a climber, the higher places had consumed him. A mountain was a selfish mistress, unforgiving and intolerant. She demanded a man's full attention. And sometimes more. Sometimes nothing less than his life would satisfy her.

That thought gave Jake pause. Just what did he think he was doing here, asking a woman like Emily to start a relationship that would never gain his full attention? She would always have to share him with a mountain. Worse, every time he went on a climb she would be left to wonder if he'd come back.

He was in a high-risk profession. One that could kill.

The gallant thing would be to stop before he ever got started with her. If his instincts were correct—and they'd never failed him yet—once he got started with Emily it would be impossible to stop. Something bigger than both of them would take over.

"Emily—"

"Shh." She put her fingers over his lips. He could tell

by the look on her face that she had guessed where this was leading. "Don't talk. Don't analyze. Please. Let's just do it."

"You're Michael's daughter, all right."

"He taught me that life's a wild, bucking bronco. The trick is to climb aboard and not get thrown off. Mother believes the same thing—she just says it differently. She says to jump and the net will appear."

Standing on tiptoe, she kissed him softly on the lips, then gave him one of the most wicked grins he'd ever seen on a woman.

"Let's get this party over with so we can cavort in the woods."

"Emily Westmoreland, I like you better every minute."

When Jake put his arms around her and led her back to the house to meet her relatives, he knew he'd crossed the Rubicon.

Emily had never in her life been one to agonize over events—past, present or future. But here she was, dressing to meet the relatives, and she was so nervous she was actually asking the advice of a skunk?

"So what do you think, Gwendolyn? Shorts and a T-shirt or the yellow sundress?" Gwendolyn sniffed around the clothes, then retreated to a spot in the sun beside the window. "That's what I thought. Yellow. Grandmother Beaufort will have a heart attack. It'll be the first time I've ever worn anything except shorts to a family reunion."

The fact was, Emily didn't give a flitter what Grandmother Beaufort thought. She was dressing for Jake, pure and simple, and the minute she saw him, she was glad she had. His eyes lit up.

"You look wonderful," he said, then leaned down to kiss her.

He was still kissing her when her brother walked into the room. Now what? She couldn't act casual, as if this was something she did every day. She didn't, and Daniel knew it. She couldn't introduce him as someone she'd brought to the reunion. She hadn't, and Michael would make that clear.

It was Jake who saved her. He slid one arm around Emily as if it were something he did every day, then held out his hand to her brother.

"You must be Daniel. Your father has told me so much about you I'd know you anywhere. I'm Jake Bean."

"The climber. I've heard of you. Welcome to Belle Rose." Daniel laughed. "Though I see my sister has already done that."

It was all smooth, effortless and completely natural. Emily thanked God for good manners and Southern upbringing and the best brother a girl could ever have. But more than that she thanked Him for Jake Bean, this perfectly wonderful man who came boldly forward and claimed her as his own.

"She has, and it was certainly the best welcome I've ever received," he said.

"You two stop talking about me as if I'm not here." Emily gave her brother a bear hug, and he ruffled her hair.

"If I were you, I'd keep him away from Edna Sue."

"Don't worry. I plan to."

"And maybe Aunt Janice." To Jake he said, "She's the nosy type. She'll ask you anything, no matter how personal." He turned to Emily. "Where are Mom and Dad?"

"Back in the kitchen, checking the food."

"Knowing them, I wouldn't bet on it." Daniel laughed. "Nice meeting you, Jake. I'll see you later."

With a wink and a smile, Daniel exited through the French doors, which led down the hall to the kitchen.

"Well..." She breathed a sigh of relief. "That turned out all right."

"I like your brother. Does it embarrass you that he caught us kissing?"

"No. I just didn't want it to be awkward for you."

"It wasn't, and it's not going to be. Even if your whole kit and kaboodle of relatives catch us kissing."

"You really mean that?"

"I do."

"You're not just saying that to be polite?"

"One thing you'll learn about me, Emily. I never say things merely to be polite. I say what I mean and mean what I say, and I don't give a hoot about convention."

Chapter Six

May 12, 2001

My children continue to amaze and delight me. Edna Sue took out after Jake, as we all knew she would. And when Emily started turning red in the face, we all knew she was going to light into her like a duck on a june bug. That would have set Mother ringing her bell like crazy, then boring us all with one of her long-winded lectures about decorum.

"Do something, darling," I said to Michael, and when he pulled that blues harp out of his pocket and did a riff, and Daniel cut loose singing "Life Ain't Nothin' But a Party," I thought Mother was going to have a conniption fit. "Lord God, Anne, your house sounds like a juke joint," she told me, and I said, "Good. I don't want any of my children to die an unlived life."

I love that phrase. Read it somewhere. I forget now. Another sign of aging, I fear.

Anyhow, back to the reunion. It was wonderful to see the way Jake acknowledged that he was with Emily. Nobody had any doubt. When he didn't have his arm around her, he was reaching out to touch her. Small things. A fingertip brushing across her cheek, a caress along her bare arm, a brief clasp of her hand.

It was wonderful to behold.

I worry about all my children, but Emily the most. Probably because she is the youngest, but in my mind she is the most vulnerable. Daniel is solid as a rock and will always be all right, and Hannah...well, all I can say is God help the person who tries to trifle with her.

But in spite of Emily's fierce independence and her brave and free spirit, she is vulnerable. There is a little girl inside her who needs taking care of.

Jake sees that, I think.

When they left together this afternoon, I said to Michael, "I just hope he will understand and cherish her," and of course, Michael knew what I meant. He always does.

"He will, Anne."

Then in typical fashion my darling husband carried me to our bed, and with the haunting strains of "Moonlight Sonata" playing on the radio, he lay down beside me and caressed me. Simply caressed me. Overwhelmed by the wonder and the beauty of it all, I pressed my face into his chest and cried.

And Michael understood that, too.

Of all the women in the world, I am the most blessed. So blessed that I'm almost afraid it's not real, that if I blink even once, it will all be snatched away.

Chapter Seven

Emily glanced in her rearview mirror for the hundredth time to be certain she hadn't lost Jake. She hadn't. He was still back there in his car, following her home.

She gave the V for victory sign, and he honked.

"I can't believe this, Gwendolyn. I'm actually taking this marvelous man home with me with the express purpose of doing deliciously wicked things with him. Can you believe that?"

Gwendolyn sighed. She'd been doing a lot of that lately. Probably she was wondering why Emily had suddenly taken leave of her senses.

The woman who was driving home wasn't the same woman who had driven to the family reunion. She was some other woman, a brave, adventurous woman who had shifted her focus 180 degrees.

Lord, what was she doing? What if he didn't like the way her cabin looked? Had she put her dirty socks in the hamper, or had she left them lying on the bathroom floor? What if he thought she was a slob? What if she snored? What if he hated the way she looked in the morning?

And worst of all, what if she disappointed him? Face it, she wasn't the world's most experienced woman. In fact, her experience had been limited to Jimmy Clark, who'd tried to show her the wonders of the flesh in the back seat of his old Chevy. Emily hadn't thought it was wonderful. In fact, she'd thought it was silly and had told him so. She'd laughed so hard he lost his ardor, and instead of sharing rousing sex, they'd ended up sharing a hot dog at Scooter's Drive-by Deli.

Lord, who did she think she was? This wasn't *Sex and the City.* It was real life. She was Emily Westmoreland, a woman who knew her way around the woods, but didn't know the first thing about men.

"I can't do this, Gwendolyn."

She put on her blinker and pulled into the turnaround, one of many on the Natchez Trace. When Jake pulled in behind her, Emily felt so foolish she couldn't even face him. Instead, she turned away and pretended to be studying the Indian mounds in the distance.

"This was once a scared burial ground."

"Emily, look at me." She felt his hands on her shoulders.

Oh, God, could she stand it? How could she look into his incredible face and say, "I can't do this."

Gently he turned her around. "Now, tell me what this is all about."

What could she say? *I thought you might want to see this historic sight?* Lord, when did she get to be such a coward?

"I'm scared," she said, looking directly into his eyes.

"Me, too."

"You are?"

"Yes."

She unclenched inside, unfolded her wings and floated upward.

"Well, then—" she smiled at him "—what are we waiting for? Let's get back on the road."

She was fixing to float to her car when Jake cupped her face and smiled down at her. She thought he was going to kiss her. Instead, he gave her the world.

"Everything's going to be all right, Emily. I promise you."

Sighing, she leaned against his chest while he caressed her hair. It felt so good that it seemed to her she'd been there forever, that somewhere, sometime, somehow she'd known him. That she'd been merely biding her time until she could find him again.

"Let's go home, Jake," she said.

As he followed her home, Jake thought about the promise he'd made. Could he keep it? It was a hero's promise. That was how Emily always made him feel, as if he were ten feet tall and invincible.

In reality he was a flawed man, quaking inside, and though he wanted to make everything perfect for Emily, perfection was rarely within the grasp of mere mortals. He would have to leave that to the gods. The most he could expect was simply this: to do his best and hope it was enough.

When Emily turned on her blinker again and he followed her through the darkening woods to the small patch of brightness where a bare bulb glowed over her front porch, Jake felt the rightness of this moment, as if he'd been running all his life trying to get to someplace he didn't even know.

At last he knew. He'd been headed toward Emily, and finally he was home.

"Welcome home," she said, then took his hand and led him inside. They kissed in the dark, and without a word she led him into her bedroom. The glow of the moon picked up a patchwork quilt, the gleam of a brass headboard, a rocking chair with an open book in the seat, a silky robe hanging over the door. Little things. Lovely things.

Their clothes fell into a heap on the floor, and Jake lay down with her on the bed. He couldn't stop touching her, kissing her. And when he entered her, he knew the whole universe was contained in that small room in her cabin in the woods.

Chapter Eight

Never had anything felt so perfect to Emily, so absolutely *right*. From the moment Jake entered her, she knew theirs was no ordinary union, but a miracle given only to those lucky enough to find true love. What was happening in her bed was more than a mating of bodies; it was a mating of hearts and souls. It was magic.

It took them hours to discover each other. And when they were finally sated, she realized the magic was still there, that even the simple act of falling asleep in his arms was a small miracle.

"Night, Jake," she murmured.

"Sweet dreams, Emily." Jake was instantly asleep, arms wrapping her tight, not letting go, not ever letting go.

And that was the miracle. The last thing you do at night and the first thing you do in the morning is hold the one you love.

Emily placed her hand over Jake's, taking his measure,

loving the way her hand seemed small as a child's and his was big enough to cover and protect. She listened to the even sound of his breathing, reveled in the rise and fall of his chest against her back. She loved the way falling asleep in his arms felt, like being wrapped in a cozy blanket.

"This is the way it should be," she whispered, but Jake didn't stir.

Emily smiled in the dark. God, she was going to love this man as much as her mother loved her father. Even more, if that were possible. The miracle of that love was filling her up, flowing through her bones, singing through her blood.

Everything she'd believed to be true about her own life was shifting, slowly but irrevocably. Emily, the independent, was metamorphosing into Emily, one of a pair, the other half of a perfect whole. And it felt so good. Oh, it felt so good.

"So this is what you do."

Jake was standing in the midst of her menagerie of animals in the compound behind her cabin. A doe with a partially healed haunch shied away behind the trees; a pair of raccoons, completely healed from the wounds inflicted by steel traps, peered at him from the brush; a red-tailed hawk tried to lift toward the sky, his broken wing flapping helplessly in the dust.

"Yes. These are my children, Jake."

"Your children?"

"They stay with me while I train them to go back into the world."

"Have you ever had any failures?"

"Not yet, though I'm beginning to lose hope for Gwendolyn. She's getting fat and content and shows no sign of wanting to return to her home in the forest."

"Maybe we should introduce her to a nice male skunk. What do you think?"

Thinking of all the things she and Jake had done under the covers last night and again this morning, Emily got hot from head to toe.

"Well, it worked for me."

Jake roared with laughter. "Are you calling me a skunk?"

"No, but you are definitely male. Exuberantly male."

He put his arms around her from behind and nuzzled her neck.

"Does that mean the lady likes me?"

"The lady definitely likes you."

And more, she thought. Ever so much more. But instinct told her it was neither the time nor the place for such confessions. Or was it?

Had her mother waited? After all, she'd said she recognized Michael as her true love almost from the minute she laid eyes on him. When had she told him? Or had she waited for him to tell her first?

Oh, Lord, why couldn't love be as simple as tending to rescued animals?

Maybe it was. Maybe all you had to do was forget about the rules and just fly by the seat of your pants. Let yourself go. Hold nothing back.

"How do you feel about making love in the woods?" Jake said.

"Now?"

"Yes, now. Any objections?"

"None whatsoever." She unbuttoned her shirt and tossed it on the lowest branch of an oak tree. "In fact, if you hadn't suggested it, I was going to suggest it myself."

They left a trail of clothes across the compound to a small grove of trees. With the fresh green leaves as their canopy and a moss-covered embankment as their bed, they entered the realm of magic that kept them enchanted for the next few hours.

"A man could get used to this," Jake said.

"So could a girl."

In fact, Emily was thinking how wonderful it would be if all her days included Jake, if she could go to sleep at night wrapped in his arms and wake up in the morning with him at her side, wake up to soft sweet kisses and delicious, lazy explorations, to the joy and wonder that comes only from being with your soul mate.

"I've never experienced such driving urges. Maybe it's the woods that encourage this primitive passion. Or maybe it's the woman."

"I like the second explanation best."

"I thought you would."

He kissed her softly on the lips, and Emily loved how it felt, as if it were an intimate ritual they performed every day and as frequently as possible. She loved that her lips were swollen from so much kissing, and still she wanted more. Jake was the kind of man she could never get enough of. The kind she'd thought she'd never find.

"How did I get so lucky?" she said.

"We both got lucky."

Jake folded his arms behind his head and stretched out full length on their bed of moss.

"Did you ever think of living anywhere else, Emily?"

"No. For one thing, my work dictates that I live in the midst of nature. For another, I've always felt that big cities have a way of stealing a person's soul."

"So have I. That's one of the reasons I spend as much time as I can climbing mountains."

"When will you go again?"

He not only climbed mountains solo, but also acted as a

guide to groups of people who would never tackle the peaks alone. He tried to screen his clients so that he took only those who were skilled and capable climbers, but many guides took clients who should never get closer than their television screen to the great mountain ranges. In fact, some of them endangered others by their dogged determination to boast of feats beyond their capabilities. There was always the possibility that one of them would slip past Jake's screening system.

Emily had learned those truths from a lifetime of living with a high-altitude filmmaker. In fact, before she'd left the reunion, her father had pulled her aside and told her the specifics of Jake's profession.

"Just so you go into this relationship with your eyes wide open, Em," he'd said. "It will take a special kind of patience to love a climbing man like Jake."

"Don't you think I already know that, Dad? After all, I've had Mom for an example."

"Yes, you have. There's no better role model in the world than your mother." Michael kissed his daughter's cheek. "Go with my blessing. I couldn't be happier if I'd chosen Jake for you myself."

"Didn't you?" she'd teased, and her father had given her that twinkly-eyed look he always got when he was keeping secrets and mighty pleased with himself, to boot.

"Never question fate, Em."

That was easy to do when you were lolling in the woods, cozy and sated, your lover beside you safe and sound. But would it be so easy when Jake was on the other side of the world and she was left behind with nothing but memories and the anxious hope that he would return?

"You didn't answer my question, Jake."

"Don't talk about when I'll leave, Emily. Let's just enjoy the time we have."

"You're right. Of all people, I should know that."

She was reaching for her clothes when Jake put his hand on her arm.

"Don't. Not yet."

That was all it took. One look. One touch. And their secret woodland bower rang once more with the sounds of their passion.

Chapter Nine

May 16, 2001

I'm in heaven. That's all. This morning when I woke up Michael was standing beside the bed with an armful of roses. "Good morning, sleepyhead," he said, and then he proceeded to strip the sheets back and sprinkle rose petals all over me. They were still fresh with dew, and I giggled like a schoolgirl when he licked the moisture away.

We didn't get out of bed till noon. I told Michael I felt positively decadent, and he said he planned to see that I felt that way from now on. Oh, it's wonderful, this retirement of his.

Such plans we have. We're going to travel, anywhere except the mountains. I've had enough of that to last a lifetime, though I don't put it in quite those words to my husband. Every time we discuss travel plans, I haul out brochures of places that have beaches and coconut trees.

He's on to me, of course. I never could fool Michael. But he pretends to share my enthusiasm for the world's tropical paradises. Yesterday he brought home a ukulele, plastic of all things, and then he serenaded me. He has a way with blues, but Elvis, he's not. He murdered "Blue Hawaii," and we both ended up rolling around on the carpet, laughing.

Of course, dear diary, you know where that led. Mmm! Delicious.

It makes me very happy to know that Emily has finally found the same thing. She called yesterday while Jake was at the grocery store to tell me how wonderful things are between them. "Everything's perfect, Mom. I have to pinch myself every morning to make sure this is not a dream."

I assured her it wasn't. I assured her it was the way true love always feels. That led to a lengthy discussion about when to say "I love you" and who says it first and whether it matters who is the first to confess.

It amazes me that people can get so caught up in rules they forget to just live. How I ever got past Mother's rules is beyond me, but I had to share with Emily how the great confession came about between her father and me. Of course, if it weren't for my diary, I wouldn't remember.

It seems Michael and I were born loving each other. It seems to me that we said it the minute we first saw each other, and that we said it at the same time.

However, my diary tells a different story.

November 13, 1966

This has been a red-letter day in more ways than one: Michael came to my house in Mississippi for the first time today, and I told him I loved him. Right out of the blue. Just said the words as bold as you please, "Michael, I love you," in spite of my mother's warnings that men never marry forward women. That's the word she used, "forward," as if I were a car that needed changing gears.

Mother was in her element giving advice before he came. "Rule number one, Anne, never kiss a man on the first date." Wouldn't she die if she knew what we did on our first date? Not even a date, really. Just a mad rush to find someplace where we could know each other's bodies as fully as we knew each other's minds and spirits and souls.

Then she went on to rule number two about the chase being all important to a man. "And never call a man—always let him call you. But the most important thing is to never, ever let on that you love him, even if you do. Play hard to get, Anne. That's the way to get a proposal out of him."

When I told her I wasn't sure I wanted a proposal, she nearly had a conniption fit. Marriage is the end-all, be-all for Mother. "What else would you want him for?" she said, as if I'd been conceived by immaculate conception.

"I'm going to be a concert pianist, Mother. I want him for companionship." Among other things that I didn't dare name. Lord, Mother would have practically barred the door if she knew all that I had in mind for Michael.

Well, Michael won her over instantly, there's no doubt about that. She practically swooned when she saw him. And charm. If he'd turned half that charm on me in the bus station, I'd have had my wicked way with him right there in the nearest broom closet.

Naturally the first thing Mother did was grill him about his relatives, who was his mama, who was his daddy, who were his ancestors all the way back to the Revolution. Mother's a member of the Daughters of the American Revolution, and puts great value on a person's lineage. Fortunately Michael's family tree is impeccable. Or perhaps not. The way his eyes were twinkling when he talked about Colonel Jeb Westmoreland and General Slim Rankin, he might have been making the whole thing up.

I was falling more in love with him by the minute.

Now, mind you, today is only the second time I've seen him, because the day after we met, he went to Alaska to apprentice on a shoot, and I got down to the serious business of practicing for my senior recital.

I graduate in December, and already I'm being courted by a professional tour group that heads to Europe in February.

Anyway, I couldn't wait to get Michael out of the living room and off to myself. The only way I could get by with carrying a quilt to the woods was by telling Mother we were going to have a picnic. And we did. Wine, cheese, fruit and bread. Home-baked. (I'm trying to impress him. I guess some of Mother's advice is rubbing off on me, after all.)

We raced into the woods and fell on each other like two naughty children. (Fortunately for us, Mississippi is experiencing another one of those beautiful autumn days that feels like summer.) Then we sat facing each other naked on the quilt, our legs entangled, pine needles in our hair, and my love for him overflowed.

"I'm falling in love with you, Michael," I said, and he held me so close I almost lost my breath.

"I don't want to hurt you, Anne. I don't ever want to hurt you." That's what he said, but what I heard was, "I love you, too."

What does it matter who says the words first? The important thing is to recognize the magic. Recognize it and welcome it home.

Chapter Ten

"You look like your mother when you smile like that."

Jake glanced up from the morning paper. He was sitting across the breakfast table from her, which gave Emily even more cause to smile. This felt like a routine they'd known and enjoyed for years, instead of only a week.

"Thank you." It was a beautiful compliment that deserved a proper response, not one of those silly disclaimers. "I have a lot to smile about." She tucked her mother's letter and diary pages into the pocket of her robe. "Namely you."

He leaned back, studying her over his coffee cup. "You make a man believe in domesticity."

Coming from one of the least domesticated of his kind, that was an enormous admission. Emily was holding her breath, hoping for more, when Gwendolyn marched into the room and wrapped herself around Jake's legs.

"Hello, girl." He leaned down to scratch her back, and she cast Emily a look that could only be called *arch.*

"Don't encourage her. She's already incorrigible."

"And still showing no signs of returning to her natural habitat."

Jake was beginning to learn her business. Just yesterday he'd been present when she released the raccoons into the woods.

"I could keep her, but then, I could keep all the animals who come into my care."

"Did you notice that black-and-white visitor we had last night?"

"No."

Jake laughed. "How could you? You were curled against me sleeping like a rock."

"It felt so good I could do it forever."

There, she'd said it. Mentioned a future with him. It was just short of a confession of love. Emily put her hand on the letter in her pocket and said a silent thanks to her mother.

Jake's only response was the small smile that played around his mouth. She would take that as a good sign.

"Maybe we should take Gwendolyn for a long walk today in the hopes of meeting our nighttime visitor." That was all he said, and she had to warn herself to slow down. After all, they'd only been together a week. Both of them were young. They had a lifetime ahead.

"That's not a bad idea," she said. "I'll get dressed."

She was down to the bare essentials and headed to the shower when the phone rang. All she heard was Jake saying hello.

Funny how one phone call could change a life.

That was what Jake was thinking as he stood in Emily's cabin in the woods listening to the sound of her shower.

Yesterday he'd stripped off his clothes and joined her. They had cavorted like naughty children.

That was one of the things he enjoyed most about Emily, her childlike joy in simple pleasures. Being with her was like discovering the world all over again. Her enthusiasm was contagious. Every leaf, every blade of grass, every star was cause for celebration to her.

He would love to stand on a mountaintop with her and show her the world.

"Jake?" She peered around the doorjamb, wet hair wrapped in a towel, simple black cotton panties clinging to her damp skin. And she'd never been so appealing to him. So dear. So important.

God, she was important. Perhaps too important.

"Who was it?" she asked.

He didn't want to tell. Didn't want to have to tell her, for the news would change everything.

Everything except the way he felt about her.

He'd never even told her, and now it was almost too late.

"James Reeves. He wants me to do an IMAX film."

"Oh?" Her smile was uncertain. "That's good, I suppose."

"Yes. It's very good. He's an excellent producer."

"Where will it be filmed?"

"Everest."

She took a deep breath. Now came the test. Would she be like all the other women he'd known? Would she dissolve into tears? Beg him to stay? Fret over the danger?

Worst of all, would she issue ultimatums?

"When will you leave?"

"Tomorrow." No tears. At least not yet. He watched her closely for any signs of resistance. All he saw was an enchanting woman with a smile on her face, a woman who somehow held his whole world in her small hands. "I have to go back to Atlanta and get my gear ready."

She faced him bravely, a small woman determined to be strong in the face of disappointment and fear. And it was there. He could see it in her eyes.

Jake closed the space between them, pulled her into his arms and buried his face in her hair. He couldn't leave without telling her how he felt. He couldn't walk away without some assurance that he would be welcomed back. He couldn't climb to the top unless he knew she would be waiting for him at the bottom.

Suddenly that was how important she was to him. She was life and breath to him. Heart and soul.

"I'll be back, Emily."

"Yes, I know." Her voice was small, muffled against his chest.

"You're everything to me." His arms trembled with the effort to hold her as close as he could without crushing her. "I never thought I'd say that to a woman."

"I never thought I'd hear it. Never even wanted to until I met you." She wrapped her arms around his chest and squeezed. "I love you so. Please be careful."

"I will, Emily. I promise."

He kissed her then and for a long time afterward. She unwrapped her hair, took his hand and led him into the bedroom. *Their* bedroom. Signs of the two of them together were everywhere, his pants draped over hers on the back of a chair, their shoes mixed together, his comb beside her hairbrush, and through the open door their toothbrushes side by side, their wet towels tangled, his shaving cream sharing space with her bath salts.

Packing up and leaving was going to be like ripping out a part of his heart. He wanted to stay here with her. Always.

And yet...they'd known each other only a week, and he

was leaving for the other side of the world. Best not to make plans. Not yet. Best to merely hold on to the moment, hold on to Emily and promise to return.

He picked her up and placed her in the center of the bed, then stood memorizing the way she looked, long, slender legs stretched out, damp hair spread across the pillow, toes painted bright red. Not her fingernails. Just her toes. Which never ceased to surprise him.

But most of all, he wanted to remember her smile. It was more than warm and inviting. It was glorious, a thing of transforming radiance. Open and innocent, and yet so intimate his heart beat faster just looking at it.

He wanted to say something to her, something she would remember in the lonely days ahead, something he would remember and be proud of. And yet she left him speechless. All he could do was lie down beside her and hold her close until hugging was not enough.

Each time they came together Emily was amazed. How was it possible for something that had started out as perfect to get better and better? She thought it had to do with the expanding of the heart. She actually felt as if her heart had grown bigger in the past week, and perhaps that was the answer. Their loving didn't get better, it merely took up more space in her body.

With her arms and her heart wide open, Emily said her long, sweet goodbye to Jake so that the next morning when he was actually standing on her doorstep with his suitcase in his hand, she didn't have a frantic urge to grab his lapels and pull him back inside. She didn't have the panic-stricken feeling of things left unsaid, deeds left undone.

"I guess this is it, Emily."

"Yes, this is goodbye. For now."

He cupped her face and tipped it up for a long kiss.

"I'll be back. Soon. As soon as I can."

"I know. I'll be waiting, Jake."

"Good. That's all I need to know."

He hadn't said words she'd wanted to hear, and yet he'd shown tenderness and loving care in a dozen ways. It was enough. For now, it was enough.

"You'll be leaving Atlanta in a few days?"

"Yes. As soon as I get my gear together and we get the film crew assembled."

"I could find someone to cover here for me. I could come to Atlanta and see you off."

"I'd rather say goodbye to you here, Emily. I want to remember you standing in the sunshine in the middle of the woods."

"I suppose this is easier. For both of us."

"Nothing about this is easy. I want you to know that."

He held her so close she could feel the rhythm of his heart against hers. She took several deep breaths, willing her heart to beat in perfect cadence with his. It was a small thing, probably silly, but she liked the idea of their hearts beating as one.

"I'll miss you, Jake. I'm missing you already."

He didn't reply, but she didn't need words. She could feel his yearning and his anguish.

If they kept on like this, she'd be crying in less than a minute, and that wouldn't do. She was absolutely, *positively not* going to cry when Jake left her. After all, he was coming back. Tears at this simple leave-taking would mark her as weak, and she wasn't a weak woman.

"I'll try to call you while I'm gone."

She knew what that meant. Dealing with overseas calls from remote places was frustrating at best. And once he was on the mountain, he'd have to be patched through, which could be a nightmare.

"As much as I'd love to hear from you, that's not necessary, Jake. Besides, I spend most of my time in the woods. I'd hate for you to go to all that trouble and then not even find me home."

He laughed. "I think I'm dreaming. Are you real?"

"I'm real. If you don't believe it, pinch me."

"I already did that."

"Oh, yeah. And I liked it. Fact is, I like everything you do."

"Everything?"

"Every little thing."

"You think you know me pretty well, huh?"

"Inside out. Top to bottom. Even that cute mole on your—"

"Don't say it, Em."

How easily they'd slipped into lighthearted banter. Just like her parents.

"Okay." She stood on tiptoe and kissed him softly. "Your secrets are safe with me."

His eyes darkened, and he crushed her against his chest and buried his face in her hair.

"Ahhh, Em." They stayed that way for a long while, swaying together, and then Jake pulled back. "If I don't leave now I never will."

He picked up his suitcase and headed to his car. *Turn back, turn back,* she silently willed him. And when he did he was smiling.

"So long, Em. See you soon."

"Yes. Soon. Bye, Jake."

She lifted her hand, and was still smiling and waving when he rounded the curve and drove out of sight.

"Goodbye, my love," she whispered.

There was a message from James Reeves waiting on Jake's answering machine when he got home. "Jake, call me. Urgent."

James was not the type to call a thing urgent unless it was. Jake could think of only two possibilities: somehow the whole IMAX deal had fallen through, or he'd decided that Jake wasn't the one he wanted to film, after all.

Jake set down his bag and picked up the phone.

"James, what's up?"

"It's Clayborn. He's down with pneumonia. There's no way he's going to recover in time to do this film."

"He's sure about that?"

"Positive. It's in both his lungs. By the time he's out of the house, we'd be contending with the rainy season. Even then, he'd be too weak to make the climb."

Jake felt almost relieved. What in the devil was wrong with him? He'd always been eager for a climb, always been chomping at the bit for the next challenge.

It wasn't Emily, as much as he was connected to her. No, it was something else. Instincts kicking in. But why?

"Then the shoot's off?"

"No. I want Michael Westmoreland."

"He's retired."

"I know that. I also know how much he likes and respects you. If you call and ask, he'll do it."

"I won't do that. I also respect him. He's made his decision to retire, and that's good enough for me."

"Just tell him about the film. That's all I'm asking."

"Why don't you?"

"Our chances are better if you do it. Besides, he was my first choice all along. You know this will be a better film with him at the helm."

James was right. Michael's work was unquestionably the best. He would make all of them look brilliant.

"Look, Jake…I'm not asking you to beg the man. Just

tell him the situation and leave it open for him to step in if he wants to. His choice.''

"Fair enough. But if he says no, I don't intend to pursue it.''

"Thanks, Jake. That's all I ask.''

Jake paced, thinking. Then he went into the kitchen, poured himself a drink and sat at the window of his apartment looking out at the darkening sky, still pondering his dilemma.

One thing was certain. There was no way he would call Jake Westmoreland without first talking to his daughter.

Emily was in the kitchen warming up a bowl of soup when Jake called. The sound of his voice thrilled her all the way down to her toes.

"Hello, Em. How are you?''

"Great. Now that I'm talking to you.''

She twirled the phone cord around her fingers and smiled.

"How was your trip home?''

"Good. A little bumpy over Alabama, but I made it.''

Small talk. But oh, it was wonderful because it was with Jake. He could read the back of cereal boxes to her and she would be enthralled. Because it was him. And because she loved him.

Nothing is insignificant about the person you love.

"How was your day, Em?''

"After you left I took Gwendolyn on that little walk we talked about, but we didn't see any male skunk suitors.''

"That's too bad.''

"I don't know. I'm getting used to her. I'd miss the little critter if she left… I miss you.''

"Already?'' She loved the way he laughed.

"Yes. I was missing you before you were even out of sight."

"I miss you too, Em."

She could hear him clearing his throat, as if he were nervous. Maybe she should steer away from that kind of talk. Especially since they were several hundred miles apart, and neither of them could do anything about all this *missing you* business.

"So, you'll be leaving in a few days?"

"There's a hitch in plans. Our filmmaker is sick and can't go."

"What a shame. Can you get somebody else?"

Jake was quiet for so long Emily thought they'd lost the connection.

"James wants me to call your father, but I won't do that if you don't want me to."

"I don't think he'll go."

"Neither do I."

"Still, he's always made his own decisions. I wouldn't presume to do that for him."

"I'll call him, then, but I want you to know I won't use any forms of persuasion on him."

"You can use your many delightful forms of persuasion on me any time you want," she said, and the conversation took a turn that left her panting...and not from the heat of the stove.

Chapter Eleven

May 20, 2001

Michael flew to Atlanta today to join the IMAX crew that will film on Everest. After Jake called, Michael said to me, "Anne, I won't go if you tell me not to."

God knows, I wanted to tell him no. I wanted to scream it. I wanted to shout the house down. I wanted to cry and roll on the floor kicking. But I've never told Michael no.

And I never will.

That's not the kind of relationship we have. That wasn't part of the bargain.

He's never denied me anything I've set my mind on, and I've never denied him. We have too much respect for each other.

"An IMAX film. And with Jake. It's too good to resist, angel."

That's what Michael told me over dinner—fried catfish fillets, which he knows good and well I can't resist, in spite of the fact that every bite I eat settles on my hips. Combine that kind of soul food with candlelight and real linen napkins, and I'm a sucker for anything he says or does.

I am, anyhow. Michael doesn't need fancy trappings to woo and win me. All he needs is his glorious self.

God, I miss him. How will I endure another lonely stretch of days until I see him again?

I'll just have to. That's all.

"I'll be back before you know it, darling," he said when he kissed me goodbye at the airport. "And then we'll go to that tropical paradise you've been talking about."

He said some other deliciously bawdy things about not getting a suntan because the sun didn't shine in the bedroom even in a tropical paradise, and I told him I would be at the airport with bells on when he returned.

Bells on and airline tickets to Hawaii in my hand.

Meanwhile I'm not even going to think about Everest. I'm not going to look at a single map. I'm not going to listen to a single weather report from the other side of the world.

I'm going to sit on the verandah sipping mint juleps while I plan our itinerary for the Hawaiian islands.

Chapter Twelve

Jake was always astonished at the power of the Himalayas to move him. From the Tibetan side the summit of Everest rose in solitary splendor, a giant totally isolated from the nearby peaks visible on the Nepal side. As he stood in the darkness looking up at the face, he felt rather than saw the person who joined him. Michael Westmoreland.

He should have known a man with such reverence for the mountains would not miss the most spectacular, most spiritual moment of the day—the dawn when nothing stirs, not even a breath of air, when the whole world stands in absolute stillness waiting for the mighty mountain to come alive.

They didn't speak. They merely stood side by side in awed silence, waiting for the sunrise. It hit the summit first, blazing across that lofty peak like fire. On the left, Lhotse's rim lit up, then the granite of Makalu began to glow. Light rolled down the mountain like a river of flame, its rose and gold tongues licking along the lesser peaks as it made its way to camp.

Neither Jake nor Michael spoke of the beauty of the sunrise. It was danger they watched, for everywhere the sun touched, moisture loosened and trickled. Small whispers at first, and then a distant rumbling that turned to the thunder of avalanches.

They roared and tumbled in the path of the sun, a stark and vivid reminder of the power of the mountain. And when the sustained roar died to an occasional growl, Jake said a silent prayer of thanks that the dangerous activity was far away from their camp.

As the first rays of sun touched the tents where their crew lay sleeping, Michael turned to him and smiled.

"What do you say we wake up these sleepyheads and get to work?"

"Sounds like a good idea to me."

They would be climbing the mountain siege-style, depending on manpower and ropes to set up a series of fixed camps from which they would operate. If there was any mountain that demanded siege, it was Everest, for she was the ultimate challenge, the climber's dream…and his nightmare.

Jake glanced at Emily's dad and wondered for the forty-seventh time about the wisdom of asking him to come back to Everest. Michael had been quick to accept the invitation and seemed happy to be back. He looked fit and trim, equal to the task. And still Jake wondered.

Would Michael Westmoreland have come back to Everest if he hadn't been the one asking?

"I can guess what you're thinking, Jake. You're wondering what brought this old man back to the mountain."

Jake didn't try to deny it.

"Not in so many words."

Michael lifted his face toward the summit. "Hear that, Jake? It's a siren song. I guess I'll always want to come back."

"But will you? Would you be here if I hadn't asked?"

"The answer to your first question is no, I won't be back. I can't do that to Anne. The answer to your second is *I don't know.* Maybe, maybe not." He shrugged. "I guess we'll never know."

"No, I guess we never will."

Michael clapped his hand on Jake's shoulder. "We're here. That's all that matters. That and telling the best damned story we can with the camera."

When Emily pulled up at Belle Rose unannounced, she told herself she was surprising her mother. The fact was, she was lonesome. For the first time since she'd been living in the woods by herself, she was lonesome. And it all had to do with Jake.

She missed him so much her teeth hurt. Her skin felt tight, as if she'd grown too big for it. And she'd developed insomnia, besides.

Her mother spotted her from the front porch and raced down the steps to meet her, arms wide open.

"Emily, what a wonderful surprise."

For an instant she thought of making up some light-hearted and witty story on the spot, but she was feeling neither lighthearted nor witty, and invention was not her strong suit. Besides, she could never fool Anne.

"I'm so lonesome I could die," she said.

"Me, too." Anne giggled. "Hey, remember that song."

Anne burst into an awful rendition of the country-and-western ballad. On purpose, because Anne Beaufort Westmoreland was a trained musician and knew her way around a ballad as well as she knew her way around a baby grand.

Emily joined in, and she didn't have to sound awful by design. Singing off-key came naturally to her, for musical talent was another of her mother's better qualities she'd failed to inherit.

By the time they got to the house, they were laughing so hard they had to cling to each other to stand up straight. Anne snatched some tissues from a box in the kitchen, which was the room they always gravitated to first.

Anne was already digging out pots. "How does popcorn sound to you?"

"With butter on top and Hershey's bars on the side?"

"What else? Soul food. Good for what ails us."

Emily perched on a stool while Anne poured oil into the popcorn pan.

"What ails us, Mother? I thought I was this independent woman who didn't want a man in my life and who certainly didn't *need* one."

"You are an independent woman, my dear. And don't you forget that."

"I'm trying not to."

"You didn't need just any man, Emily. You still don't. But a special man, a soul mate…that's a different story. And therein lies the difference between the mundane and pure magic."

Anne poured kernels of corn into sizzling grease, and as they bloomed, the smell filled the kitchen, Emily thought of being at the circus and believing in magic.

She'd been six, instead of twenty-four. Still, the seeds of magic had lain dormant all those years. It had taken only one glimpse of Jake to make them spring to life.

As the rising corn began to lift the lid off the pan, Emily melted the butter. They poured their soul food into an enormous bowl, then went onto the west verandah where they could watch the sunset while they licked butter off their fingers.

"What do you suppose they're doing now?" Emily asked.

"They should be close to the summit by now. Getting ready to wrap up the film and come home."

"You think so?"

"I know so. I always keep track, Emily, whether I mean to or not. Something deep down inside me knows."

Here at last was a trait Emily would inherit from her mother. Instinctively she knew that. As the weeks turned into months and the months to years, she would develop some internal clock that told her exactly when Jake would be coming home.

That was how her mother had kept track, and that was how Emily would. She wouldn't need to mark off days on the calendar. She wouldn't need to watch the clock. She would simply know.

"I can hardly wait," she said.

"Neither can I."

They dipped their hands into the bowl and exchanged a soft, secret smile.

As the IMAX team made progress up the mountain, Jake understood why Michael was considered the best high-altitude filmmaker in the business. His keen cinematic eye combined with his ability as a climber kept the shoot moving along at a steady pace. There was no time wasted on filming useless footage. Michael had a vision that swept them all toward the summit.

Jake was outside early the morning they were to gain the summit, and as usual, Michael was already there staring up at the peak.

Jake stood quietly beside him while the sun lit the face of the mountain.

"Awesome, isn't it," Jake said.

"Yes. People who have never seen this wonder why we climb. What do you tell them when they ask, Jake?"

Jake had reached the summit ten times. Today would be the eleventh. And each time he stood more than 29,000 feet above the rest of the world, he was filled with a sense of hope unlike any he'd ever experienced. A sense of rebirth and renewal. An overflowing of passion for life.

He never felt he'd conquered the mountain, but that he'd joined it, become one with nature. Standing on the summit of Everest was the closet thing he knew to understanding and spiritual awakening.

"I tell them that gaining the summit is a symbol of hope and a celebration of the human spirit."

Michael put his hand on Jake's shoulder and squeezed. "So do I," he said. "So do I."

They gained the summit in spite of the fact that they'd lost their assistant cameraman to high-altitude sickness. Danny Clemmons had departed for base camp the day before. Following the route used by Sir Edmund Hillary and the Sherpa Tenzing Norgay, they pushed through the mists without him until they finally emerged at the highest peak in the Himalayas.

Not even the sound of Michael's camera whirring could take away Jake's feeling that he was alone on the top of the world.

His face deeply burned from snow and sun, his emotions raw, his body pushed to its limits, Jake stood there, awed and exhilarated. The first thing he would do when he got back home was share his feelings with Emily. She would understand. He knew that instinctively.

"It's a wrap," Michael said. "Let's go home."

They made their descent to camp in the growing darkness. But even so, the vast plume arising from the top of Everest, caused by two masses of air, one warm and one cold, colliding, showed that the wind velocity had picked up.

Jake was glad to be descending. He didn't relish the idea of being caught near the top of the mountain in a storm.

The avalanche caught them unaware. Exhausted from their long climb and exposure to both high altitude and the elements, they were sleeping the next morning when the first onslaught of rocks and snow hit their tents.

Gauging by the thundering roar, Jake figured the avalanche to be a mile away, Everest releasing its fury. With the avalanche so far off, there was no risk of being buried alive. The only danger was from the flying debris driven by a giant wall of air. With everyone still inside sleeping, they would be relatively safe.

As Jake rolled himself into a tight ball for the onslaught, he saw a lone figure outside, camera in hand.

"Michael!"

He had no more than yelled the name when a storm of snow and flying rocks blotted out everything except the sound of the mountain's passing fury.

The pounding against Jake's tent sounded like baseballs being thrown full force against canvas. He couldn't see anything. Not even his fingers in front of his face.

There was nothing he could do now except hunker down and wait until the wall of snow passed over them. The minute the roaring ceased, he was up and running.

"Michael's out there," he yelled, and two Sherpas emerged from their tents, also running.

They found him facedown, a tiny stream of blood turning the snow red.

"Michael! Can you hear me?"

There was no answer.

"Turn him over. Gently now...gently."

With the help of the Sherpas, Jake turned Michael over and cradled his head in his lap. Blood oozed from a head wound, coloring Jake's hand and staining his clothes.

"Michael...Michael. It's Jake. Can you hear me?"

Nothing but silence. Deathly silence.

Jake's chest constricted and tears clogged his throat. How was he ever going to tell Emily?

Chapter Thirteen

"Noooo!"

The scream jerked Emily out of sleep and propelled her from the bed.

"Mother!" She grabbed a robe on her dash toward her mother's suite. By the time she'd gained the hallway all she could hear was the harsh sound of sobbing.

Anne was huddled on the bed, hands over her face, shoulders shaking with the force of her pain. Beside her lay the telephone receiver.

"Mother, what's wrong?"

"Oh, God, no-no-no-no."

From the neglected phone came faint sounds. Emily picked it up.

"Hello?"

"Emily?" It was Jake. Emily wrapped her arms around herself to ward off the chills that went through her. "Thank God...Emily."

"Jake, what's wrong?"

"It's your dad, Em. He got caught in an avalanche."

Emily cupped her mouth to keep from adding her screams to her mother's anguished moaning.

"Is he—"

"No. God, no, Em. He's not dead. He's in a coma. Except for that, he's in good shape. No broken bones, no bruises except the one on his head where he got hit."

Emily sat on the bed and put her arm around her mother. In moments of crisis she'd always depended on Anne…and Michael. Now she had no one to depend on except herself.

"Mother and I will fly out. Where are you?"

"We're in Chengdu, flying out to Chongquing tonight, then on to Hong Kong in the morning. Meet us there."

"Jake, how bad is he?"

"The team doctor is with your dad, Em. He says it's hard to tell in cases like this."

"He'll come out of this, won't he?"

She didn't like the way Jake hesitated. "Jake, is there something you're not telling me?"

"No, I've told you everything I know. Naturally, we expect him to come out of it. Have you ever seen anything keep Michael Westmoreland down?"

Emily could spot false cheer a mile away, and she loathed it.

"I'm not a little girl, Jake. You don't have to paint a pretty picture for me."

"Sorry. I didn't mean to be doing that. I just don't want you thinking the worst."

The worst, of course, was that Michael had gone into a deep sleep from which he would never return. Days would turn into weeks and weeks would turn into months, then years while they stood at their father's bedside watching him dwindle away, watching him leave them by degrees.

"No," she said, "I won't think the worst. All the Westmorelands are positive thinkers. By the time we get to Hong Kong, Daddy will be up in arms about us flying halfway around the world over nothing."

"You're exactly right."

Emily held on to the phone, waiting for Jake to say more, but the gulf of silence only widened. Emily felt as if she were on a boat drifting slowly away from Jake. Part of her wanted to call out to him, but part of her wanted to disappear over the horizon into blessed oblivion.

Right now she didn't want to deal with all the feelings attached to a new relationship. She didn't want to deal with a passion that simmered underneath the surface, even in the face of disaster. She didn't want to deal with longings of the soul and cravings of the body. She didn't want to deal with *need*.

"Emily…"

"Yes?"

"I'll take care of everything from this end, the hospital, the hotel. Everything. You just get the plane tickets and I'll meet you at the airport in Hong Kong."

Chapter Fourteen

June 25, 2001

I have this sense that I'm in the middle of a bad dream and I can't wake up. I want to run away from this place, this sterile hospital room where my husband lies with his arms crossed over his chest sleeping like a child, but I can't get my legs to move. My body feels too heavy for them.

Everything about me feels too heavy. My arms, my face, my heart. Oh, my heart. Sometimes I think I can actually hear little pieces of it separating from the whole and falling to the floor. The sound is like Mother's fine china that day I told her I was moving in with Michael and she said, "Over my dead body. You will not leave this house, young lady, do you understand?" I picked up the china she prized more than anything, and threw it as hard as I could. I wanted to hurt her.

That's the way I feel now. I want to hurt somebody. My husband doesn't move, doesn't talk, he doesn't even blink his eyes, and I want somebody to blame.

I'm afraid Emily's already assigning blame. It's not Jake's fault, I told her, but she wouldn't believe me. She's stubborn that way. Just like her father.

Sometimes I could shake both of them. I might even try that with Michael. Wake up, I'll say. You're scaring me. And he'll come out of this awful sleep laughing and hugging me close and kissing my nose the way he always does when he's played a prank on me.

But this is no prank. Yesterday when we got here I went straight to the bed and wrapped my arms around him and said, "Michael, it's me, Anne. I love you, darling. Wake up. Please, please wake up. For me. Do it for me."

He has never in his life refused me anything I want. I know he would respond if he could. He wouldn't go off and leave me like this. Stranded. A woman without a home.

Michael is my home. What do I care about Belle Rose? Without him it's just a pile of bricks with a roof on top.

I asked Jake if Michael said anything after the avalanche hit, if he moved, if he made any sign, any sign at all. "No," he said. "I'm sorry, Anne. There was nothing. He was exactly as you see him now."

It's not fair. People don't just go off and leave you without a word. A gesture. Something. Something to cling to. Some little shred of hope.

I will not give up. I refuse to. Michael is going to come out of this. He will.

Because I love him. Because he loves me.

Chapter Fifteen

Emily hadn't said anything about placing blame, but Jake could feel it simmering beneath the surface just the same. How could she not blame him when he blamed himself?

Michael Westmoreland would never have been on Everest if Jake hadn't called him. It was that simple.

And now that the crisis was over, now that the long trek down the mountain was over, now that the agonizing journey out of the Himalayan villages with Michael still as death was behind them, Jake had nothing to occupy his mind except regret and self-recrimination.

Emily sat on the edge of a straight-backed chair in the hospital's waiting room with her arms wrapped around herself. Jake sat facing her, not knowing what to do, what to say.

They felt like strangers to each other. How could that be after the passion they'd shared? Why weren't they sitting side by side with his arm around her, her head on his shoulder? Why didn't she say something? Cry? Accuse him?

Anything. Anything at all except this frightening silence.

She hadn't even said anything to him at the airport, not really. Nothing personal. Nothing of significance. Just the basics. *How's Dad? Where is he? How long will it take to get to the hospital?*

What did all this mean in terms of their relationship? Was this her way of saying *I don't want you anymore?*

Maybe she was wondering the same thing about him. When he'd met them at the airport, he'd taken Emily into his arms, but she'd pushed quickly away. And so, not knowing what to do about her, Jake had done nothing.

"Emily?" When she looked up, her face was devoid of all expression, almost as if she were seeing a stranger. "I'm sorry about your dad. I'm sorry all this happened."

"I appreciate your saying that, Jake."

So cool. So remote.

"I heard the avalanche coming, Em. I saw your dad standing outside, but it was already too late. I yelled at him, but he never even heard me."

She bolted to the window and stood with her back to him.

"I don't want to hear about it. All right? I don't want the gory details."

"I was just…" Jake faltered, uncertain. The truth hit with the force of the avalanche. He was losing her. He was losing her as surely as he'd lost Michael.

He joined her and stood quietly for a while, staring at the hustle and bustle of Hong Kong beneath the window. Then he put his hands on her shoulders. She suffered them there, stiff and unyielding.

"There was nothing I could do, Em.

I'd give the world if I could change things, but I can't."

"I'd give the world, too...if I had him back." She hunched forward with her arms wrapped around her waist. "I want Dad back."

He felt the tremor that ran through her, sensed rather than saw her tears. Jake turned her around and pulled her into his arms. At first she resisted. And then she melted against him and wet his shirt with her tears.

Relief flooded him. He wasn't going to lose her, after all.

"Everything's going to be all right, Em."

He rubbed her back and caressed her hair while she cried soundlessly against his shoulder. And when her tears ceased, she lifted her face to him, and he bent down and kissed her softly on the lips.

"Yes. Everything's going to be all right," she said. "Do you have a handkerchief? I never have one when I need it."

He pulled one from his pocket, then wiped her face with all the tenderness that was in his heart.

"Now," she said, "let's go in and see Dad."

"You want me to come, too?"

"Yes. Please."

She wrapped her arms around him, and Jake's world righted.

When Emily walked into the room where her father lay, the first thing that struck her was how natural he looked, as if he'd fallen asleep watching a ball game. His color was good, his breathing sounded normal, at least to her untrained ears.

"Mom?" Emily spoke quietly, the way you do when you don't want to wake somebody from a well-deserved rest.

Anne sat beside Michael, holding his hand, and if anybody had asked Emily which of her parents was sick, she'd have said Mom. Her dark eyes looked enormous in a face drained of all color.

"Any change, Anne?" Jake asked.

"No, none. And both of you speak up. I want Michael to hear you." Anne turned to her comatose husband. "Darling, Jake and Emily are here. Wake up so you can talk to them. They want to talk to you, Michael. Open your eyes, darling."

Her father didn't stir. Anne leaned close and brushed his hair back from his forehead. "Squeeze my hand, darling. Just to let them know you hear them."

He didn't move, didn't acknowledge their presence in any way.

The hope Emily had recaptured in the safety and comfort of Jake's embrace began to fade.

"Come over here, Emily, and touch your father. Rub his hand. Let him know you love him and want him to come back to us."

Jake squeezed her hand, then gently nudged her toward the bed. Why was it so hard for her to approach her father?

"Dad?"

Up close she could see the difference between normal sleep and a coma. Michael's stillness was complete, his body totally inert.

"I'm here, Dad. I love you."

His hand was a dead weight in hers, lifeless. Emily fought back tears.

"You come over here, too, Jake," Anne said. "I want you to tell Michael about the film."

Jake stood close behind her, and Emily took comfort from his nearness, his body heat. On the heels of her comfort came the guilt.

Jake stirred feelings in her that all of a sudden felt wrong, out of place, totally inappropriate in light of the situation. She had to escape. She needed to think. She needed space. She needed air.

"I don't think Dad's warm enough, Mom. Why don't I go down to the nurses' station and get another blanket?"

"That's a good idea."

When Emily left the room, Jake was telling Michael that the IMAX film was safe and already in post production. Just as if they were having a normal conversation.

Oh, God, it felt awful to think of her father as helpless. Michael Westmoreland had always been the strength of their family, the rock that sheltered all of them, the beacon that always brought them to safe harbor.

Where was her safe harbor now? When she'd been in the woods with Jake, she'd thought of him in that way. He was home to her, safe harbor, shining beacon.

And now she felt it all slipping away. She didn't want it to. God knows, she didn't want to lose that, too. And yet already the absolute certainty she'd once felt with Jake was eluding her.

She would get it back, that was all. Somehow she would reclaim those feelings.

Leaning against the wall, she took deep, steadying breaths. A nurse passing by on her rounds hesitated in front of Emily.

"Are you all right, miss?"

"Yes, I'm fine."

She wasn't, of course. At the moment Emily wondered if she'd ever be fine again.

When she returned to her father's room with the blanket, Anne was at the foot of the bed massaging Michael's feet, and Jake was standing by the window looking anxious.

"There you are," Anne said. "Hannah called while you were gone. She was going to fly to Hong Kong, but I told her we'd be going back to the States as soon as the doctor okays a transfer.''

"When do you think that will be, Mom? Have they said?''

"Probably another day or two. Daniel wants to fly over, too, but I told him Jake would see us safely home. Besides, Michael is going to be awake by then.''

How easy her mother made it all sound. It wasn't lack of intelligence that made Anne so confident in the future, but a deep faith and a strength that Emily was only beginning to guess at.

Anne covered Michael with the blanket, then moved to the head of the bed and kissed him softly.

"Aren't you, darling? Aren't you going to wake up in time for our trip back home?''

Beyond the window, lights pierced the veil of darkness that had enveloped the city, artificial lights so bright they blotted out the stars. All of a sudden a wave of homesickness hit Emily. She wanted nothing more than to be standing outside her cabin in northeast Mississippi gazing up at Venus blazing over the deep woods like a promise.

It wasn't the place so much as the state of mind she longed for. That feeling of knowing the ground beneath her feet was solid. That nothing in her life had shifted out of focus. That tomorrow would be as safe and secure as all the days that had gone before.

Emily reached for Jake's hand and held on tight.

"Anne,'' he said, "I'll take you and Emily back to the hotel whenever you're ready.''

"No. I'm not leaving Michael. You two go ahead.''

Jake held Emily close in the back seat of the cab, and she didn't say a word all the way back to the hotel, just leaned bonelessly against him, trusting and sweet. They stayed that way, wrapped up together in the elevator all the way up to her room.

He didn't ask if he could come in. It wasn't necessary. The awkwardness of the past few hours had vanished, and when they walked into her room, she stood in his arms kissing him as if he were a soldier recently returned from war.

"Oh, God, I've missed you, Emily."

"Shh. Don't talk, Jake. Just hold me. *Hold* me."

They kissed until their lips felt bruised, and then they lay down together, fully clothed, and caressed each other. Simply caressed.

He didn't speak. Didn't dare. Words might shatter the spell.

And surely this was a spell they were under, the same bit of magic that had overtaken them in Mississippi. With the blinds closed against the sights and sounds of Hong Kong, they might have been at her cabin in the woods, instead of in a strange hotel in a foreign land. With the door shut against the world, they might have been in a time before the avalanche, a time when there was no doubt about their future together.

He slid her blouse from her shoulders and buried his face in the soft mounds of her breasts. Her scent was sweet to him, like roses after a rain; her skin, familiar, its silky texture a balm to his battered soul.

He reveled in the touch of her, the taste of her, until his blood was racing like a storm-gorged river.

Still silent, they cast their clothes aside and came together with the fury of two storm fronts colliding over the peaks of Everest. There was nothing soft and sweet about their joining. Their need was too great for gentleness, their passion too-long-denied for tenderness.

Quite simply they devoured each other. The minutes

turned to hours and still they were not sated, still they were not spent.

In the midst of their furious lovemaking, Jake had flashes of insight, his mind clear and detached, lucid as a bell. It seemed to him they were trying to deny the truth with their bodies, that they were seeking to wipe out the accident with the sheer force of their mating.

He drove into her ceaselessly, and she matched him with an abandon that took his breath away. Repeatedly he brought her to screaming climax. Repeatedly she arched high against him, went slack, then urged him forward once more.

Jake astonished himself. He was performing Herculean feats that would daunt men ten years younger. Emily's power to do this to him put him in awe.

She was a sorceress, and in the arena of the bedroom he bowed willingly before her.

But what about afterward? Would this power turn against him? Could it break him?

Jake pushed the thought aside. He was with her, inside her, and nothing else mattered. Not yesterday, not tomorrow. Only the here and now.

He wrapped her legs around his neck and tasted deeply of her, feasted on her honeyed warmth until she was begging for release once more. Heaving and sweat-slickened, Jake drove into her until he was finally beyond control.

He called her name, and as the floodgates of passion opened, she gave a shattered cry.

Afterward they lay against each other, spent. The night turned cool, and when Jake reached over Emily to pull up the covers, she didn't even move.

Tenderly he wrapped the blanket around her, then lay there wide-eyed, holding the whole world in his arms.

Chapter Sixteen

Emily awoke, momentarily disoriented by the strange room and the time difference. She sat up, taking the covers with her.

The bedside clock radio told her she'd only slept four hours. She should be exhausted, but she wasn't. She was filled with a strange energy. Restless energy. Nervous energy.

"Em?" Jake reached up and pulled her back into his arms. "What's the matter?"

"Couldn't sleep."

"Mmm." His hands began to move over her in slow, lazy caresses.

She allowed his touch. More than allowed it; she wallowed in the pleasure of it. A jolt of guilt caught her unaware.

How could she do this? How could she lie in bed with Jake making love as if nothing had happened? How could she be happy while her father was in a coma and her mother was in pain?

She started to pull away, but Jake held her fast.

"Don't go, Em," he murmured. Sleepy. Sexy.

Emily was powerless to resist. Didn't want to. Didn't have any choice in the matter. Already he was parting her thighs. And when he slid inside she felt such a sense of completeness, she wept. The tears rolled silently down her cheeks and wet the sheet she held knotted under her chin.

This was so right. So perfect. And yet...

Don't think, she told herself. It's still dark. You can't do anything to help your father and mother in the middle of the night.

As the slow and lazy rhythm increased, Emily forgot everything except desire, which grew and grew until there was no room inside her for anything except passion. She abandoned herself to it, embraced it as the only sure thing in her life.

Jake rolled onto his back, taking Emily with him, and she rocked above him as fiercely as if she might stop the world with the sheer force of her lovemaking. Suspended, she forgot everything except the storm of emotion that swept through her.

On the way to the hospital that morning, Emily played games with herself. If she didn't think about anything except her father during the cab ride, he would be all right. If the clouds had vanished by the time they reached the hospital and the sun was shining, he would be out of the coma. If she promised God and Grandmother Beaufort to give up her maverick ways and become more like her mother, Michael Westmoreland would miraculously awake.

"Em? What are you thinking?"

Sitting in the cab in the harsh light of early morning,

Jake had the look she'd seen in her father when he returned from his mountain adventures: weathered and wise, as if the glare of sun and snow had not only parched his skin, but had burned away everything extraneous in his life, leaving nothing behind except truth and a soul on fire.

Emily caught her breath and put her hand over her hammering heart.

"Em? Are you all right?"

"Yes, I was just…just thinking about piano lessons."

"Piano lessons?"

"Yes, I never did try to learn to play. All those lessons and all that money wasted. Why did I do that?"

"I don't know." He caught her hand and squeezed. "Is it important?"

"Everything seems important right now. It's almost as if…I don't know how to say this. Maybe if I had been different growing up, none of this would have happened. Maybe I didn't try hard enough."

Jake looked as if he'd been gut-punched.

"Em, don't. If anybody's to blame, it's me."

"No. I don't blame you."

Don't you? She wanted to put her hands over her ears to shut out the voice.

"I blame myself," he said.

Suddenly there was this monster between them, a giant hairy thing taking up all the space, breathing all the air so that Emily felt shrunken. She felt as if all the life had been sucked out of her.

She wished she'd never mentioned her guilt. She wished she'd kept her thoughts to herself. She wished she'd talked about the weather. Anything. Anything at all except the one subject that was guaranteed to drive them apart.

"Hospital," the cabdriver announced, in broken English,

and Emily had never been so relieved to reach her destination, in spite of what awaited her inside.

Although she and Jake walked side by side up the long flight of steps to the wide front doors, she felt as if they were on separate planets. They were both silent in the elevator going up to the third floor, both trying not to look at each other.

But she couldn't help herself. Jake caught her stealing a glance and gave her a tight smile. Forced. Artificial.

She smiled back. What actors they had become.

"Maybe there'll be good news waiting for us," he said.

"Yes. Mom was very optimistic last night."

The doors slid open and they walked down the long, white hallway, not touching. Being scrupulously careful not to touch.

Emily told herself she was distancing herself from Jake for her mother's sake. She told herself she didn't want anything to remind her mother of her own loss.

But when she walked into room 308 where her father still lay in a coma, she could no longer avoid the truth. Her love for Jake, a love that had been born in sunshine, could no longer survive the harsh light of day, for during the waking hours a powerful spotlight was trained on their guilt.

A single traumatic event had banished them to the darkness. Only under cover of night did Emily feel free to love Jake.

Her mother sat beside Michael's bed exactly where she'd been the day before, holding his hand. If it hadn't been for her wrinkled blouse and the mussed cot beside the window, Emily would think she had sat there all night.

"Any change, Mom?"

"No. None." Anne drew herself up, drawing strength from some unknown source. "Who knows what the day will bring, though? I expect Michael to be coming awake any minute. He doesn't like to miss out on things."

She turned to her husband and smoothed his hair back from his forehead. "Do you, darling? You're missing all the fun, you know. Emily's here. And Jake. Just think of all the places the four of us could go together. Open your eyes, darling. Please. Do it for me."

Emily never could keep a straight face. Her brother used to tease her and say, "You'll never be a professional gambler, Em, that's for sure. You could never have a poker face."

She felt her face crumbling now. Any minute she was going to start bawling like a newborn calf.

She felt Jake's hand on her shoulder. How easy it would be to lean back against him and receive the comfort he offered. But even that small gesture seemed like a betrayal of her mother. And her father.

She moved to stand beside the window. Jake's face gave away nothing as he moved to the opposite side of the room.

On the bed her father lay still as death, and beside him, Anne looked like a woman turned to stone. If that picture didn't change within the next few minutes, Emily was going to start screaming.

"Mom, Jake and I are going to wait in the hall while you shower and change, and then he's going to take you somewhere for brunch."

"I'm not leaving the hospital. Besides, I already ate."

There was a half-eaten pack of nabs open on the cabinet in the corner of the room.

"I can see that you did." Emily jerked up the nabs and threw them into the garbage can. "At this rate, I'm soon going to have *two* parents in the hospital."

"I'm fine. You two go and get something to eat. I'll stay with Michael."

"No. *I'm* staying with Dad, and *you're* going to go somewhere and have a decent meal."

Anne opened her mouth to protest when Jake intervened.

"We won't leave the hospital, Anne. There's a decent cafeteria downstairs."

"It's settled, then." Emily took Jake's arm and headed toward the door. "Take all the time you need, Mom. We'll be just outside."

"Ten minutes. That's all I need."

"Great."

The minute they were out the door, Emily dropped Jake's arm. He didn't say anything, just waited beside her until Anne opened the door.

"Come in, Emily. I want you to sit beside your father the whole time I'm gone. Hold his hand and don't let go. And talk to him. He needs to know we're here."

"Don't worry, Mom."

Emily sat down and picked up her father's lifeless hand.

"Good. Massage it. It'll help keep up his circulation." Anne bent and kissed Michael softly on the lips. "Bye, darling. I'll be back before you know it."

The first time Emily had ever seen a life-size dummy in a wax museum, she had screamed. She'd been six, and terrified.

She wasn't six anymore nor was she terrified, but her father's hand felt as if it belonged to a wax figure. It wasn't real. It didn't close around hers, protecting, guiding.

Emily escaped to the window. How could she possibly have a conversation with her dad? That wasn't him in the bed. That was a lifeless body with a mind in suspension.

That stranger had nothing to do with Michael Westmoreland, who had read all the Pooh stories to her and taught her to ride a bicycle and tutored her in the multiplication tables. He had nothing to do with the man who was tall enough to put a star on top of the Christmas tree without standing on a ladder, but not too tall to bend down to listen to a child.

Emily leaned her head against the cool windowpane while tears trickled down her cheeks and made crooked patterns on the glass. When the phone rang, she jumped.

"Hello?"

"Emily, is that you? Where's Mom?"

It was Hannah, her older sister who had always been larger than life to Emily. The sister she'd tagged along behind, trying to stretch her legs so she could step precisely into her footprints. The sister who had ended Emily's childhood by telling her there was no Santa Claus, and who, years later, had initiated her into womanhood by telling her what a first kiss felt like.

"She's gone to get a bite to eat."

No need to mention Jake. Hannah would ask a million questions, then proceed to dispense advice. The last thing Emily needed right now was sisterly advice. Even if the sister was the usually fabulous Hannah.

"How's Dad?"

"Still the same, Hannah. He's just…lying there."

"Oh, God, Em…I didn't even come to the family reunion."

"All of us understood why you didn't come."

"*Couldn't* come, not *didn't*. Anyhow, that's not the point. I thought I'd have years. I thought, with the retirement he'd always be there when I got home."

"For Pete's sake, Hannah! Dad's not dead."

Silence. Emily could hear Hannah breathing, and then her soft inquiry.

"Can Dad hear you?"

"I don't know. Mom thinks he can."

"Then don't say things like that!"

Suddenly it was all too much for Emily—her father's accident, her mother's heartache, her lover's slow drifting away.

"Don't tell me what to do, Hannah. Don't you dare tell me what to do!"

"Hey, all right. I'm sorry. I know how hard it's been for you, Em. I should have come to Hong Kong."

Emily wiped her face with the back of her hand. "No, it's all right. Really. Mom and I are making it just fine. Anyhow, the doctor says we can go back to the States in a few days."

"In a few days Dad's going to be all right?"

"No. I didn't say that. I don't know, Hannah. The doctors don't know. Nobody knows. We'll just be going home, regardless. That's all."

"I'll have this Amazon story wrapped up in a few days. I'll come home as soon as I can."

Relief washed over Emily. When Hannah came home, she would share the burden.

"I'll be glad to see you, and I know Mom will."

"Good. Tell her I'm coming home. And, Em…tell Dad, too."

After she'd hung up, Emily sat in the chair beside the bed looking at her father. Although the huge round clock hanging on the wall was electric, she could swear she heard it ticking.

"Dad?" She called his name softly. "Are you there?"

There was no response whatsoever. Not even a tremor of his eyelids.

"I don't know if you can hear me or not. I hope you can because there are some things I want to tell you. First, Hannah's coming home. She wants you to know that. She loves you, Dad. And I do, too. We all do."

Emily's bottom lip started trembling, and she bit down to stop it. Tears were a luxury she could no longer afford.

"I know you're planning to come back to us, but I want you to know that until you do, I'll take care of Mom. If I'd said that two weeks ago, you'd have laughed your head off and told me she was strong enough to handle a hurricane single-handedly. And I'd have said, yeah, Dad, you're right."

Emily leaned close and smoothed the cover over her father's chest. Then she repositioned his hands, lacing the fingers together the way she'd seen him do so many times.

"I'm the only one living close enough to be there for her. And I promise you I won't let anything stand in my way."

Not even Jake.

She wondered what her father would say if he knew that she and Jake were having trouble. What advice would he give? Would she ever know?

She leaned down and kissed him on the cheek. "Rest now, Dad. Get strong again. And then come back to us. Please."

Jake had sensed the change in Emily this morning in the taxi, and it had been even more obvious when he and Anne came back from breakfast.

Now he and Emily were back again in her hotel room, and they might as well have been in different cities. That was how wide the gulf between them had grown.

Jake found it almost unendurable. He'd never before faced a situation he didn't know how to handle.

Emily stood at the window in her silk pajamas brushing her hair and looking out at the night-lit city as if she couldn't get enough of the view.

"Emily?"

She didn't turn around, not even when Jake stood behind her and put his hands on her shoulders.

Look at me, he wanted to say. Instead, he took the brush from her hand and ran it through her hair. A few strands escaped the bristles and wrapped themselves around his fingers. A silky caress.

Jake had to have more. Weaving his free hand into her hair, he began to massage her scalp. Only then did Emily start to relax.

Such a small thing. His hand in her hair. And yet, hope doesn't require much encouragement.

He laid the brush on the windowsill and caught her hand.

"Come to bed, Emily."

She let him lead her to the bed they'd shared, if not eagerly, then at least willingly. He turned back the covers and when she climbed in beside him, he took her in his arms and began to kiss her.

She allowed his kisses. That was the kindest way to describe it.

"Em?"

"I'm sorry, Jake."

"Hey, there's no need for you to apologize. I understand."

Only too well.

The gulf between them became an ocean. And Jake didn't even have a paddle, let alone a canoe.

What would he do if Michael were not in a coma? What would he do if he was back in Mississippi where the deep woods surrounded them and the owl's cry sounded through the darkness?

His hands found the small of her back, and he began to caress her. Softly. Tenderly.

She didn't move, didn't make a sound. Maybe touching her wasn't such a good idea. Jake took his hands off her and was preparing to roll over and try to get some sleep when she spoke in the faintest of whispers.

"Please. Don't stop. That feels so good."

He drew her close and began to caress her once more. Giving. Not taking. Not expecting anything in return. Merely giving.

"Jake?"

Her breath was warm and sweet against his neck.

"Hmm?"

"Will you hold me like this all night?"

"Yes."

"Just hold me."

It wasn't everything Jake wanted, but for now it was enough.

Chapter Seventeen

June 30, 2001

We got home yesterday—Jake and Emily and Michael and I. Though I really can't say I've brought Michael home. Just his empty shell. This body that doesn't move and doesn't speak.

Does he hear me? Does he know me?

The doctors say he does. They say that on a deep level the patient in the coma understands everything that's happening around him.

That's why I've brought his favorite CDs and a portable player to the hospital. There's a song by T.Bone Walker playing now, "Stormy Monday Blues." I keep expecting Michael to get out of bed, grab his harmonica and play along. He always does that. Feet tapping. Body swaying. He says it's impossible to sit still when T.Bone's wailin' the blues.

Well, he was wrong. He's not moving now.

Will he ever move again? Will he ever play his harmonica? Will he ever grab me in a bear hug and dance around the room?

I have to believe he will. If I don't I'll go mad. Believing I'll soon have Michael back is the only way I can get through the day.

Last night when I played Tony Bennett for him—"Time after Time"—I said, "Do you remember that song, darling? Squeeze my hand if you do."

I waited and waited. Surely he would respond. Surely he remembered. How could he forget?

Tony Bennett had been singing that song when Michael proposed to me. I'll never forget it. We'd gone dancing to celebrate my graduation from Juilliard.

The band was good, the dance floor small, the lighting intimate. It was a night for celebration. Not just my graduation, but my invitation to be part of a three-month concert tour in all the major cities of the U.S. and Michael's first solo job. He'd been assistant director on high-altitude films many times, but never director.

A proposal was the last thing I expected.

We were dancing close, making love on the dance floor, he called it. And all of a sudden he said, "Marry me, Anne."

I laughed. Didn't think he was serious.

"Sure," I said. "I've known from the minute I met you that someday I'd marry you."

"Not someday. Now."

"You're serious, aren't you."

"Why wait? Unless you want a big wedding."

"Oh, just a big production and fifteen hundred of my closest friends." He laughed then, and I said, "I just want you, Michael. That's all."

Three days later we were married by a justice of the peace, much to Mother's mortification.

"A JP!," she said. "I'll never live it down."

She did, of course, because she loves Michael. How could she not? He's the most wonderful man in the world.

I squeezed his hand while Tony Bennett crooned on the portable CD player and begged him, "Please, please remember, darling."

If he was ever going to respond, that was the time. Suddenly I felt the slightest movement, hardly more than a tremor. But something. Oh, God, at least it was something.

I was so excited I called the nurse.

"Michael moved," I said to her, but I could tell she didn't believe me, so I told him, "Darling, do it again. Squeeze my hand."

Nothing happened.

"Please, darling, show me you can hear me."

The nurse gave me this look, then patted my shoulder as if I were four years old.

"There might be involuntary tics from time to time," she said. "I don't want you to get your hopes up."

What's life without hope?

"Every person on this staff should have his hopes up," I told her. "Not merely for Michael, but for every patient in this hospital."

Was I wrong to tell her that? I don't think so. It seems to me that hope can do as much to heal as medication. Probably more.

I don't know how I would ever get through this without hope. And without my family.

Emily and Jake are at the airport now picking up Hannah, and Daniel will be here tomorrow. I'm glad they're coming home, more for Emily's sake than mine. She's been with me through this whole thing, and quite frankly I'm beginning to worry about her.

She was at the hospital this morning at six o'clock. By herself. She said she'd come to make sure I had a good breakfast, and when I asked her where Jake was, she said he was still in his room sleeping and she hadn't wanted to disturb him.

"What do you mean, in his room?" I asked her, and I could tell that she hadn't meant to let that slip out. The fact that they were in separate bedrooms.

I could tell things weren't right between them when we left Hong Kong, but I'd hoped that coming home would help. I'd hoped that once they were back in familiar territory, the pull of shared memories would right whatever is wrong between them.

"You can't let what has happened to Michael change things for you."

That's what I told her early this morning. Of course, she pretended she hadn't. That's Emily for you. Always wanting to make sure everybody else is comfortable and satisfied, even if it means sacrificing her own happiness.

She's a natural-born caretaker. I guess that's why she chose the profession she did. She tries to rescue people the same way she does animals, without a thought for her own needs.

I'm afraid that's what she's trying to do now. Rescue me by sacrificing herself.

I don't know how much longer Jake will stay in Mississippi. Long enough, I hope, for him and Emily to patch things up.

Maybe having Hannah home will help. She was always my practical child. Plus, she's a born leader, and Emily has always idolized her.

It won't take her long to get the lay of the land, and when she does she'll set Emily straight.

Oh, I know I worry too much about my children. Michael always said that. And he's right.

He should be my only concern now.

He looks so natural lying there, almost as if he's dozed off and will wake up any minute and be himself again.

Having him so close and not being able to hold him, really hold him, is agony. And why not? Why can't I climb in bed beside him and hold him? Not just for my sake, but for his.

Maybe full body contact will trigger something in him, some deep primitive need that will shake him out of his deep sleep and bring him back to me.

That's what I'm going to do. Tonight after the nurses have made their rounds, I'm going to shut the door and climb in beside him and wrap my arms around him and say, "Hold on to me, darling. Don't let go. Hold on long enough to want to come home."

Chapter Eighteen

Emily had really wanted to pick up Hannah by herself. But here she was sitting in the car, next to Jake, on a collision course with disaster. That was what it would be when Jake and Hannah met. A full-fledged catastrophe.

Why hadn't she had enough backbone to say, "Jake, I'm going to pick up my sister by myself?" Why hadn't she had enough courage to tell Hannah about him on the phone, prepare her a little?

She was a coward, that was why. She didn't like confrontation, and she certainly didn't like hurting people's feelings. That explained part of it.

Things had been bad enough with Jake when Emily had insisted on separate bedrooms. It was late, she'd told him, and they were both exhausted from the long flight. Plus, she wanted to get up early and go to the hospital without disturbing his sleep.

Little white lies.

And Jake had let her get away with them. He'd kissed her on the cheek and told her to sleep well. They'd both pretended everything was all right.

Emily wanted it to be the truth. Didn't she?

Going to the airport alone would have compounded their problems. But it certainly would have simplified things with Hannah. It would have given Emily a chance to prepare her sister.

Now it was too late. She and Jake stood side by side as stiff and uncomfortable as two fence posts, and any minute now Hannah's plane would be landing.

Jake put his hand on the small of Emily's back, then withdrew it. Emily's already frayed nerves unraveled another notch.

"What's your sister like?"

"Bold, beautiful and bossy."

"She's like you, then, except for the bossy part."

"I'm not a bit bold."

"Don't sell yourself short, Emily."

"Can we talk about something else?"

"The weather? That's always a safe topic."

Jake's voice held an edge she'd never heard. Emily's first impulse was to take issue. She was spoiling for a fight, anyhow. All she needed was a target.

"Yes. It's the old standby for people who have nothing else to talk about."

"Is that us, Emily? Two people with nothing else to talk about?"

She wanted to snarl *yes*. She wanted to snap at him like an angry little cocker spaniel so he'd go away.

There. She'd thought it. She wanted Jake to go away. She had too much else to deal with, not the least of which was a sister who would not only ask hard questions, but who would demand answers.

If Jake went away it would simplify things for Emily. Recently she'd discovered she was the kind of woman who could only handle one situation at a time.

But if he left her, then what? Would he come back? Would she want him to?

She glanced at the face that had become so dear, the lips that were so familiar, the eyes that had a way of seeing straight through to her soul. And all of a sudden fear socked her so hard her knees nearly buckled.

"I'm sorry, Jake. That was totally uncalled-for."

"You're under a lot of pressure, that's all."

"That's no excuse for rude behavior. Besides, you've been so good to us."

He wasn't touching her. If they'd had this conversation a month ago, Jake would have been massaging the back of her neck or running his hands down the length of her back.

But that was BC. Before the coma.

Now everything had changed. Something inside Emily shattered.

Oh, God, I can't stand this.

She reached for his hand, and when he laced his fingers through hers, she could have wept with relief.

"Hold on, Jake," she whispered. "Don't let go."

"I won't. I promise."

Emily didn't know how long they stayed that way. She let herself forget about time. She let herself forget about everything except the two of them standing there with hands joined and hearts full of yearning.

Then suddenly Hannah was striding through the doorway, and Emily's first thought was, *I'm caught redhanded.*

Self-consciously she let go of Jake's hand. Hoping Hannah hadn't noticed. Hoping she wouldn't hurt Jake all over again.

"Emily." Hannah caught her in a bear hug, then leaned back to study her. "It's been rough on you, hasn't it."

"It hasn't been nearly as hard for me as for Mom."

Apparently Hannah didn't even realize that Jake was with her. Emily couldn't keep postponing the inevitable. Taking a deep breath, she made quick introductions.

Hannah gave him a piercing scrutiny, but she didn't say anything. Thank goodness. And thank Grandmother Beaufort for drilling them in manners.

Hannah would not make a public scene. In Grandmother Beaufort's book, that was a cardinal sin.

A lifted eyebrow was Hannah's only signal that she wanted answers.

"Jake was with Dad in the Himalayas when the accident occurred."

"We appreciate your sticking around to help out the family," Hannah said.

Now it was Jake's turn to give Emily a puzzled I-want-answers look.

"I wouldn't be anywhere else," he said.

Then he staked his claim. That was all Emily could call it. His arm slid around Emily's waist in a gesture that was both possessive and somehow intimate, a gesture that clearly defined their relationship.

And Hannah was nobody's fool. For a split second she looked as if she were ready to start firing questions, then she changed her mind.

"Let's get my bag and get out of here," she said. "I want to see Dad."

She turned on her heel and strode ahead of them. Stalked, really. A tigress of a woman with a flowing black mane, green cat's eyes and long legs.

Beside her sister, Emily always felt like a clumsy midget.

When the crowd separated them from Hannah, Jake leaned down and said, "Don't let her intimidate you."

"I won't."

"Good."

He tightened his arm, and this time Emily didn't pull away. Furthermore, when she got a chance to be alone with him, she was going to make up for her coolness.

"Over here, Emily," Hannah called. "I've got my bag. Let's go."

Emily amended *when* to *if*. *If* she got a chance to be alone with Jake again.

Jake could see the tension in Emily. Her smile was forced, her face stiff. Even her skin looked tight. Part of it was due to her father, of course, but he knew that wasn't all.

He was partially to blame. Was he making matters worse by staying? He could only stay a few more days at best. He had a job to do, clients waiting. He couldn't stay in Mississippi indefinitely.

His heart sank. He didn't want to leave Emily until they had resolved their problems. But how could they resolve them if they couldn't even talk about them? And how could he resolve problems in his relationship when he couldn't even resolve problems within himself?

"I'll leave you two at the hospital and pick you up later. I'm sure you and Anne have lots of family business to discuss."

"Fine. Thanks, Jake." Emily leaned over and gave him a sisterly peck on the cheek.

It was better than nothing.

Jake stayed in the parking lot until Emily and her sister had disappeared through the hospital doors, then he turned the car back to Belle Rose, back to the place that had once held magic.

Would it ever know magic again?

Hannah and Emily didn't talk on the way to their father's room, but there was a certain tension between them. They'd always been friends, closer than most sisters with a four-year gap in age, but it seemed to Emily that somehow recent events had driven a wedge between them, and the fracture was growing wider by the minute.

She tried to think of something to say that would make things better, but she kept coming up blank.

The door to Michael's room loomed before them, and Hannah leaned against the wall and closed her eyes.

"I don't know if I can do this. I don't think I can go in there and see Dad helpless without crying."

Suddenly the breach between them closed. Emily slid her arm around her sister's shoulders.

"It's all right to cry, Hannah."

"No. Dammit, it's not all right to go in there and act like a weakling. Mom needs me to be strong."

"You're right, but a few tears aren't going to mark you as weak. They'll only show that you have a heart."

Hannah took the tissue Emily offered. "When did you get so wise, little sister?"

"Oh, life has a way of doing that to us if we'll let it." She linked arms with her sister. "Let's go in and see Dad."

Hannah didn't cry. She went straight to Anne and held her for a very long time, saying, "Everything's going to be all right, Mom," and then she leaned over the bed and kissed her father.

"Hi, Dad. It's me. Hannah. I'm home, and I brought pictures. You should see what they're doing to the Amazon rain forest. It broke my heart." She dragged a chair close, then sat down and held Michael's hand. "I want you to wake up now, Dad. I need you to tell me that my stories and photos are going to make a difference. I need you to tell me how brave I am to follow the stories to the world's hot spots and how proud you are of me."

Discouraged, she glanced at her mother. "Keep talking, Hannah," Anne said. "I know he wants to hear the sound of our voices. It may be the only thing that will pull him back to us."

"Remember when you used to tell me I'd never be happy unless I was traipsing around the world following the hard stories? You were right, Dad. It seems I'm exactly like you, always taking risks. I guess that's why you went back up that mountain. You couldn't resist one more challenge."

Emily put a restraining hand on her sister's shoulder, but Anne beat her to the punch.

"Don't upset your father, Hannah."

"I won't, Mom. I promise." She kissed Michael one more time, then relinquished her chair. "Rest now till you're ready to come back to us." To Anne she said, "Turn up the music please. There are some questions I want to ask."

Blues by Memphis Slim had been playing softly when they entered the room. Anne turned up the volume, then motioned for Hannah and Emily to follow her into the far corner of the room.

"Let's go into the hall, Mom," Hannah said, but Anne vehemently shook her head.

"I won't leave Michael."

"You don't even go home at night?"

"That's right."

"You're going to wear yourself out."

"What if he wakes up in the middle of the night and I'm

not there?'' Anne shook her head again. ''No, I won't leave him.''

''He won't have to be alone. We can take turns staying.''

''It's no use to argue, Hannah,'' Emily said. ''I've tried that. Mom's doing what she thinks is best.''

''All right, then.'' Hannah turned her laser eyes first on Emily, then on her mother. ''I want to know exactly what he was doing up that mountain.''

''Making an IMAX film,'' Anne said.

Emily could see that she would say no more.

''I know that, Mom. What I want to know is why he was there in the first place and what this Jake character has to do with it.''

Hannah wasn't fooled, and she'd never be satisfied with less than the whole truth.

''His name is Jake Bean,'' Emily said, ''and I don't want you ever to refer to him again in that derogatory fashion.''

''Emily, Hannah, if you're going to argue, go home. I don't want to hear it and I don't want Michael to hear it.''

The door burst open.

''Which one of these rowdy women do you want me to straighten out first, Mom?''

''Daniel!''

He swept them all up in his hugs and his perpetual good humor.

''I didn't think you were coming until tomorrow,'' Anne said.

''I caught an earlier flight.'' His smile was infectious. ''And just in the nick of time, it seems.''

Chapter Nineteen

It was dark when the three Westmoreland siblings got back to Belle Rose, and Gwendolyn was the first to greet them. She clambered off the front-porch swing and sashayed down the steps.

"Good grief," Hannah said. "What is that skunk doing here?"

"Her name is Gwendolyn, and she's happier here than in the woods." Emily bent to stroke Gwendolyn's soft fur.

"I might have known." Hannah said.

"I couldn't very well leave her in the woods crying while I went to Hong Kong, now could I?"

"Don't tell me you carried her to Hong Kong with you!"

"No. But I did consider it."

Hannah and Daniel burst out laughing, and he said, "Life with the Westmorelands."

"It's a sitcom," Hannah said. Sobering, she added, "Sometimes."

"Everything's going to be all right." Daniel draped an arm around each sister and hugged them close.

"I said that, too, but I don't really believe it."

"That's the difference between you and me, Hannah. I do."

"Yeah, but you've got a hotline to a higher authority, little brother."

"So do you, Hannah. All you have to do is pick up the phone."

"Pass the collection plate, Emily, while I render a song." Hannah began singing "Bringing in the Sheaves," and the three of them went into the house together, laughing.

The laughter was still with them at the dinner table, and Jake found himself watching it with a sort of envy. He'd never had brothers and sisters. Didn't know what it was like to share private jokes, to go into gales of laughter over something other folks wouldn't even find amusing, to tease and fight and argue and know that in the end it would all work out fine because this was family.

He could be part of this family. That was what he wanted. To sit beside Emily at the Westmorelands' dinner table and be included in all the inside stories. To smile at her across the table over a glass of wine and know that within an hour the two of them would walk up the stairs and share a bed in Belle Rose because that was where they belonged. Together.

Suddenly Hannah focused all her attention on him.

"So tell me, Jake. What was my father doing out in that avalanche while the rest of you were sleeping?"

The laughter stilled, and Emily tensed as if she were caught in the crosshairs of a rifle. Jake would have reached for her hand, but she was on the other side of the table. He gave her a reassuring smile, then turned to face the inquisition he'd known was coming from the moment he'd met Hannah at the airport.

He was glad it had come at the dinner table, glad she had chosen to quiz him, instead of Emily. At least he could spare Emily that.

"Michael and I had been in the habit of getting up before the rest of the crew. We liked to watch the sunrise."

"So why weren't you out there?"

"Hannah…" Emily said.

"It's okay, Emily. I'd want to know if I were in her shoes."

At the head of the table Daniel was sitting quietly, watching and waiting. It was a benevolent sort of silence, and Jake found himself liking Emily's brother more by the minute. She had told him Daniel was one of the youngest men ever to become senior pastor at a big-city church, and Jake could see why.

"We'd finished the climb, Hannah, and I was exhausted. I didn't even know Michael was out there until the avalanche woke me up."

"Wasn't there something you could do?"

"Nothing. By the time I called out to him, it was already too late."

The daughter of a seasoned climber, Hannah understood the nature of the avalanche without further questions. Jake leaned back in his chair, thinking it was all over.

Then Hannah proved him wrong.

"He was on that mountain because of you, wasn't he?"

"Hannah. Don't." Daniel's rebuke was mild, but Emily turned pale.

"Stop this right now." Emily shoved back from the table and stood with her fists balled on the white tablecloth. "If you want to place blame, place it on me. I'm the one who told Jake it was all right to ask Dad to go."

"But would he have gone if it had been anybody besides Jake who asked him?" Hannah threw her napkin onto the table and stood to face her sister. "It seems you've rescued more than one skunk, Emily."

"Enough." Daniel towered over his sisters, and it wasn't anger that commanded their attention but the powerful beneficence that radiated from him. "We will not assign blame in this house, and we will not let this tragedy divide us. We've always stood together as a family, and we will stand together in this."

"You're right, Daniel," Hannah conceded quickly and gracefully. Turning to Jake, she said, "I'm sorry. I was rude and out of line, and I hope you'll forgive me."

"Apology accepted."

Across the table Emily was still pale and shaken. Jake wanted to put his arms around her and comfort her, but decided that would only exacerbate the situation.

"Em?" Hannah smiled at her sister. "Forgive me?"

"Always, Hannah. We're sisters."

"And on that happy note, I think I'll take myself off to bed. It has been a very long day." Hannah stood on tiptoe to kiss her brother on the cheek. "What would we do without you, you old teddy bear?" Then she waved two fingers at Jake and Emily. "Night all. I'll see you in the morning, and I'll try to behave."

Daniel laughed. "I'll see if I can get the Boss Man working on that, Hannah."

"Ha. I didn't say I *wanted* to behave, just that I'd try."

"Ice cream, anybody?" Emily asked, and then disappeared into the kitchen, happy, it seemed, to have a small task to distract her.

"I'm sorry for all that," Daniel said to Jake after his sisters had gone.

"It's not a problem."

"Nobody blames you for what happened."

"They don't have to. I blame myself."

"I'd like to talk to you about that, Jake, but right now here comes Em with our ice cream." He got up from the table and took the tray from his sister. "Mmm. Three scoops of chocolate. Looks good, Em. Thanks."

"I'm so glad you're home, Daniel."

It wasn't what she said so much as what she did that betrayed her feelings. The smile she gave her brother wavered.

Jake's heart broke for her. It broke for both of them. She was close to the edge, and there didn't seem to be anything he could do to help her.

They ate their ice cream and then went into the den and sat for a while. Daniel did most of the talking. About his work, mostly. And about Atlanta, a city so big and impersonal that two people could live there for years and never even know each other until a tragedy threw them together.

The conversation began to wane and Daniel suggested a game of chess, but Jake could tell his heart wasn't in it. His heart was in a spare white room where a giant of a man lay perfectly still, slowly drifting away from his family.

It was Emily, though, Jake was most concerned about. She'd lost weight. The color and fire seemed drained out of her. He wanted to take her in his arms and hold her close. He wanted to feel her heart beating against his. He wanted to touch the satin of her skin and the silk of her hair. He wanted to kiss her once more, to slide into her soft, sweet body and possess her.

But he had somehow lost the right. He'd had the whole world in his arms, then he'd let it slip away.

"I'll take a rain check on that chess, Daniel," Jake said.

"I think I'll turn in, then. You two probably have a lot to talk about."

Daniel kissed his sister's cheek, then shook Jake's hand and left the two of them sitting as still and silent as bookends. Not knowing what to say. Not knowing what to do.

"I'm sorry about Hannah's outburst," Emily finally said.

"Don't be. She was just being honest."

"Still…"

The room suddenly seemed as vast as the Sahara, with Emily on one side and Jake on the other. And nothing between except endless sand and killing winds.

"You don't have to stay here, you know," she said.

"Are you saying you want me to go?"

"No. It's not that. I just don't want you to feel obligated. With Daniel here and Hannah, there's nothing, really, to keep you from your work."

"Yes, there is, Emily. There's Michael. And you."

"Dad's going to be fine."

"What about you?"

She shrugged, smiling, but he could see how strained her smile was.

"I'm always fine. The Westmorelands are made of strong stuff."

Was the declaration of independence her way of saying she would manage just fine without him? And why was he sitting there like a lump without asking her? Why couldn't he open his mouth and say, "Let's get all this out in the open"? Why couldn't he say, "Our relationship is stalled, and I want to get it back on track"?

The answer, of course, was guilt. It seemed to Jake that as long as Michael lay in a coma, all of them were in some ways suspended.

The best thing to do would be to say good-night so Emily

could go to bed and get some rest, and then hope that the morning brought good news.

She was watching him with an air of expectation. What was it she wanted? What was he supposed to do?

Jake was furious at his own feelings of uncertainty. He'd never been in a situation when he didn't know what to do. Maybe what was happening to them was merely fate's way of saying, *I told you so.*

All his instincts had warned against getting involved in a game that had no rules.

"I should say good-night," Emily said. "I want to get to the hospital early tomorrow."

"I thought perhaps Hannah would go. Or Daniel, so you could have a little break."

"Hannah is going, but I'm going with her. The gardenias are in bloom, and I want to pick some while the dew is still on them. Mom and Dad have always loved the smell of gardenias. I thought the fragrance..."

She covered her hand with her mouth, trying to cover the little break in her voice, but Jake heard it, anyway. It propelled him across the room, and he pulled Emily into his arms.

"They say that smell is a powerful trigger for the memory. Gardenias might be just the thing to pull Michael out of his coma."

"Do you really think so?"

"Absolutely."

She leaned against him in the old way, and for a moment Jake believed they would be all right.

"Jake..."

"What, Em?"

Suddenly the softness went out of her. Jake felt as if he were holding a cardboard doll.

"Nothing." She stood back and gave him a brave smile. "Good-night, Jake. I'll see you in the morning."

"Night, Em."

He stayed downstairs a long time after she left, trying to decide what to do. At midnight he was no closer to a solution than he'd been at dinner, and so he went upstairs to bed. Being careful not to look at Emily's closed door.

Chapter Twenty

July 14, 2001

I slept with Michael last night in his hospital bed, thinking it would make a difference. Thinking he would be aware of me. Thinking he would wake up in the middle of the night and say, "Oh, there she is," then reach for me and rouse me slowly from sleep with little kisses all over my neck and shoulders. The way he always does.

Did.

Michael doesn't do that anymore, and I'm so mad I don't know what to do. I want to kick these walls down. I want to jerk that tacky clock off the wall and throw it at the nurses who keep telling me, "The longer he stays in a coma, the less his chances are of coming out."

Don't they know I won't let that happen? Michael won't let that happen. He won't stay asleep and leave me to go on without him. Alone. A half-woman. A woman who might as well curl up beside him and go into a coma herself if he doesn't wake up.

I had such high hopes for last night. Was it foolish of me to try to rouse Michael with passion? That's what I did. And I wasn't subtle about it, either. Never mind that the night nurse could have come through the door at any minute for just about any reason.

I lay under the covers with my husband and put my hands on him and whispered the words he loves to hear. And hoped for a miracle.

Prayed for one.

"Please, please, please." I said the words over and over again as if God had suddenly gone stone deaf. Or at the very least, hard of hearing.

When nothing happened I got so mad I snarled, "All right, have it Your way." Lightning didn't strike me dead. That's what Mother always said. "Anne, if you curse God, lightning will strike you dead."

I waited. Truly, I did. When I felt a cramp in my arm, I thought Mother's prediction was coming true. By degrees. God wasn't going to wipe me out in one fell swoop, but little by little.

Then I realized I was the cause of my own cramp. The bed is narrow. Too narrow for two people.

Why do they design hospital beds that way? It's so lonely. Wouldn't the patient be far better off if somebody he loved could sleep with him every night? If somebody could hold his hand and whisper, "Don't worry, I'm right here next to you and nothing bad is going to happen to you"?

That's what I told Michael after I tried to rouse him so outrageously. "Hang on," I said. "As long as you hang on to me, nothing can tear us apart. I won't let it."

It seemed he did just that. Hung on. As if he'd tightened his grip. As if he'd had a grip to tighten.

Or did I just imagine it? Sometimes late at night when fears crowd in with the dark, my imagination plays tricks on me.

I dozed a little last night. I hadn't meant to. I had meant to stay awake all night and work at bringing Michael back to me. I was going to force him to come back with the power of my love.

But it didn't work that way.

Or did it? Sometime in the middle of the night I felt that familiar sweet-hot touch in what my husband has always called the love cradle. (Oh, I know it's not very original, but it is certainly something you'd expect of a man in love with the blues and familiar with the explicit lyrics of the likes of Mississippi John Hooker and Tampa Red.) I felt his hand on my thigh moving in that soft, erotic way that always drives me wild.

I clawed my way out of sleep, still fuzzy-headed but reaching for my husband. Calling his name.

He didn't answer me. Didn't move.

But there was his hand on my thigh. Just as I'd dreamed. Just as I'd hoped.

Had I put it there? Or had he?

I wrapped my arms around him and put my face right next to his and asked him. "Did you touch me, darling? Tell me you did. Please, Michael. Talk to me."

He didn't, of course. There was not a single sound except the drip of the sink's faucet in the corner of the room.

I hadn't drawn the curtains because we've always loved lying in bed together watching the moon. (I thought that, too, might rouse Michael from his deep and disturbing slumber.) His face was so wonderful in the moonlight, high cheekbones, squared jaw, eyebrows still dark as crow's wings, beautiful mouth. (Oh, God, that beautiful mouth. The things he could do with it...)

I had to stop a while and cry. I'm feeling better now. Maybe I should do that more often. Cry. Just let it all hang out.

Anyhow, back to last night.

As I lay there watching Michael's face, suddenly I saw tears on his cheeks. He's crying, I thought. He's crying for me.

Then I realized I was crying, too, leaning over him so that my tears fell on his face. Were the tears on his cheeks his or mine?

I wish I knew.

Chapter Twenty-One

"You brought them!" Anne buried her face in the gardenias Emily and Hannah had brought to the hospital by the armful. "There's nothing like that smell."

It was the first genuine smile Emily had seen on her mother's face since before they'd left Belle Rose for Hong Kong. It made getting up at the crack of dawn to behead the gardenia bushes worth the effort.

"Where shall we put them, Mom?" Emily asked.

"Everywhere. Michael's going to wake up today. I just know. And when he does I want him to see flowers everywhere he looks."

Emily started arranging gardenias on the windowsill, while Hannah took up her vigil by the bed.

"Dad," she said. "It's me. I want to talk to you. It's important."

Emily kept arranging flowers, concentrating on making her father's surroundings look more like a florist's shop than a hospital room. The flowers smelled wonderful and camouflaged the scent of sterility. They made you think that any minute now guests were going to walk through the door in their fancy clothes and a party would kick into full swing.

"Please, Dad. Wake up."

Emily couldn't look. She didn't want to see her father's still, white face, her sister's despair, her mother's anxious hope.

"What do you think about this?" Emily asked.

She'd put some of the gardenias in those little individual plastic containers florists use for shipping, and now she stood with her back to her family stuffing the flowers around the wall clock all of them hated. One by one they'd stared at it ticking off the minutes and hours and days of this strange suspension.

"Anything is an improvement," Hannah said. "Here, let me help."

"Emily, why don't you come over here and say something to your father?"

"Let me just get these gardenias arranged first."

"Hannah can do that."

Emily felt like a prisoner being led out to the brick wall to be shot. Every time she saw her father, she heard her own voice on the telephone. Talking to Jake.

Sure, tell Dad you need him on Everest. Tell Dad. Tell Dad.

She'd give everything she owned to take it all back. She'd give a million dollars, if she had it, to relive that moment. Just that one moment.

She would say to Jake, "Don't you dare mention a mountain to my Dad. He's through with that. After all those years he made it safely home. Let him alone so he and Mom can finally have some time together."

They were together, all right. But in a hospital room where the only thing they shared was the air they breathed.

Anne leaned over the bed and brushed Michael's hair back from his face. It was getting long. Emily wondered if they should bring in a barber. Would the doctor allow that?

"Look, darling, here's our Emily." Anne motioned her daughter to come closer, then whispered, "Take his hand, Emily. He likes that."

How do you know? she wanted to shout. *How can you tell?*

"Hi, Dad." She reached for his hand, picked it up, lifeless and waxlike.

And suddenly the monitors went crazy.

"What is it? What's happening?" Anne leaned over her husband. "Michael? *Michael.*"

The door burst open and a nurse came running to the bedside.

"Out of the way."

Emily squeezed between the nurse and the wall, but Anne wouldn't go that far from Michael. She went to the other side of the bed and hovered anxiously there, saying over and over, "What's happening to my husband? Please, tell me what's happening."

"Code Blue! Code Blue!" The hospital's speaker system blared out the chilling answer to Anne Westmoreland's question.

Her husband was dying.

Jake thought long and hard before he decided to talk to Emily's brother. He liked Daniel. It wasn't that. The problem was that he didn't know whether to approach Daniel from a professional or a personal standpoint.

In the end Jake decided to play it by ear. He found Daniel in the den browsing through the bookshelves.

"Daniel? I hope you don't mind if I join you."

"Not at all. I was just looking for a good book to take with me when I go to the hospital this afternoon. If I can I'm going to talk Mom into coming home and letting me stay there tonight."

How easy Daniel made it all sound. How natural. As if he were planning for a picnic in the park.

"There's something I've been meaning to talk to you about."

"Good. Have you had lunch yet?

"Not yet."

"Let's go scavenge in the kitchen. I think there's a pizza in the icebox and I know there's beer in the fridge. Talk's always easier with food."

Over beer and pizza, all Jake's reservations vanished. It was no wonder that Daniel had risen through the ranks so quickly. He was one of those rare people who not only put you immediately at ease, but who gave you his full attention. He had a way of listening with his head tilted and his eyes alight, and he exuded a warmth that invited confidences.

Daniel didn't prod, didn't push. He merely waited for Jake to open up. And finally he did.

"I suspect you know what this is about," he said.

"I can guess, but I'd rather hear it from you."

"This is not about Emily. Let me make that clear. Whatever happens between us will be strictly our own doing."

"As it should be." Daniel smiled. "Besides, Em doesn't take kindly to interference in her life. Even from her well-meaning brother. Can I offer a word of advice, though?"

"Certainly, but at this point I think it'll take more than advice. I think it will take a miracle."

Daniel laughed. "I can't help you there, but I know somebody who can."

"Put in a good word for me, then, would you? I need all the help I can get."

"You probably don't need as much as you think you do. Now, about Em...don't rush her and don't push her. She may not look like the fiercely independent type, but underneath my baby sister's lovely fragility beats the heart of a tigress."

Jake smiled. He'd seen that tigress firsthand, both in and out of bed.

Would he ever see it again?

Until the matter pressing on his mind was resolved, that question was moot.

"I came to you to talk about Michael."

"Yes. I gathered as much."

"The bottom line is, he wouldn't have been on that mountain if I hadn't called him. He would still be with his family if it weren't for me."

"There's a certain logic in what you're saying. My dad is in a coma and somebody has to be blamed. So you're the logical one, because you made the call and you were there. Right?"

"Right."

"Wrong. Nobody is to blame. Dad's accident was caused by an act of nature, which can be either benevolent or fearsome, but is never personal. If you have to cast blame, rail against an impersonal nature. Which, by the way, is totally out of your control."

"That's one way of looking at it."

"As for Dad being there, it was his decision. He would never have gone back unless he'd wanted to. Maybe he wouldn't have gone back so soon if it hadn't been for the IMAX film, but sooner or later he would have gone back. Perhaps to a fate even worse."

He clapped Jake on the shoulder. "If you want absolution from the Westmoreland family, you have it. I don't blame you for Dad's condition, and neither does anybody else in our family."

"Even Emily?"

"Most of all, Emily. I think what's happening with the two of you is life's problems getting in the way of romance." Daniel laughed. "And by the way, I like the idea of you romancing my baby sister. I know you had Dad's approval, and you have mine, too."

"Thanks, Daniel, but it takes two to make a romance, you know."

"Never having been down that primrose path, I don't. I'm what's known as that rare beast, an eligible bachelor." Daniel's big booming laugh filled the room. "I reckon the Lord's got other plans for me right now, or else he'd put somebody in my path besides Susie June Crump."

"Who's that?"

"The organist. A pillar of the church. Wears so many pink ruffles on her clothes you wouldn't be able to tell one end of her from the other if it weren't for her bleached-blond corkscrew curls."

Jake roared with laughter. "I can picture her. The earnest type?"

"Extremely. She gushes for about ten minutes every Sunday about my sermons. Even quotes me. Sometimes I suspect she's taking notes... More pizza?"

"Don't mind if I do." Jake delved into the box. "Have you ever done any climbing, Daniel?"

"No. Never wanted to. I played a little baseball in high school and college. Wasn't very good at it. I guess I'm the bookish type."

"I'll bet you're hell at Scrabble."

"Yep. Don't mind bragging."

"I'm pretty good myself."

"You shouldn't have said that. Wait right there. I'll get the board."

Daniel came back in a few minutes, and they set up the board on the kitchen table.

"Prepare to have your socks beat off," he said.

"Never issue a challenge to a man who's been to the highest peak in the world."

"Why?"

"Beating you has now become a mission."

Daniel laughed. "Careful there. You'll be treading in my territory."

They were well into the first game when the phone rang. Daniel picked up the receiver.

"Hello...Emily...Emily, slow down," he said. Then, "I'll be right there."

He hung up the phone and turned to Jake.

"It's Dad. They called a Code Blue."

"I'll go with you."

"Thanks."

As they raced to Jake's car, he asked. "How bad is it?"

"I don't know."

Chapter Twenty-Two

"Daniel's on his way," Emily told her sister and her mother.

The three of them hovered in the hallway outside the room where frantic activity swirled around Michael Westmoreland. Hannah had her arm around her mother, as much to keep her from rushing back into the room as anything, while Emily was terrified and trying not to show it. Probably the only thing that kept her from falling apart was that Dr. Larry Crane was in the room with her dad. Bald, brilliant and kind, he was not only the best doctor on staff but an old family friend.

Emily had raced to the phone as soon as the Code Blue was called, and now she questioned Hannah about their father.

"What's wrong with Dad? Did you find out?"

"Pneumo thorax is what Dr. Crane called it. Collapsed lung."

Emily glanced at Anne's pale face, then asked the question, anyhow. "How bad?"

"Nobody knows that yet, Em."

"Did I cause it?"

"God, no. What makes you say that?"

"I don't know. He was fine, then I picked up his hand and everything went crazy."

"A rapid pulse rise is the first signal. It had nothing to do with you. With any of us. Let's just hope Dr. Crane got there in time."

"He got there in time," Anne said. "I would know if..."

She fell silent, but both her daughters understood what she was saying. Anne's bond with Michael was so strong that if his heart stopped beating, hers would know.

"Mom."

Daniel strode toward them, big, confident, full-of-faith Daniel with Jake in tow, and all of a sudden the world seemed a brighter, more hopeful place. Emily's brother had always made her feel that way, and yet today it was Jake who held her attention. Jake whose presence pulled at her like a magnet. Jake whose face was the one Emily most wanted to see.

The realization came as a shock. She'd felt so empty standing in the hallway, so alone. The sight of Jake changed all that. It gave her a sense of standing on solid ground once more. A sense of having found something she hadn't even known she'd lost.

He came and stood quietly at her side. Not touching. Not saying anything. Just being there.

Emily wanted to reach out and touch his hand. *I'm here,* her touch would have said. *I care.*

And she did. That much she knew.

The part she didn't know, the part that scared her out of her wits was the future. What was going to happen to them next? And how much of it depended on her father? How much depended on her, on Jake?

Emily didn't know, and she guessed it was the uncertainty that held her back.

For now, though, she didn't want to think about it. She simply wanted to be in the moment, to be fully there, her best and strongest self so that all of them—Michael, Anne, Hannah, Daniel and most of all Jake—would know that she was a woman, whole and complete, and that no matter what happened she would survive. No. Not merely survive. She would triumph.

Standing among the tense family, Jake felt all his guilt come back. Daniel's theories notwithstanding, he sensed that if he didn't leave soon, he would bring an even greater calamity on the heads of this family, who had been nothing but kind to him, nothing but generous.

What would Michael Westmoreland say if he knew he'd taken a viper to the family's bosom? Unfortunately it looked as if he would never say anything.

Dr. Crane came to the door, and the family crowded around him. Jake stood back, close enough to hear, but not close enough to signal him as a part of the family.

An outsider. That was what he was, after all. And getting more so by the day.

"How is he?" Anne asked.

"The worst is over. I inserted a chest tube, which will reinflate the lung."

Hannah and Emily started talking at once, but it was Daniel's quiet voice that was heard above the rest.

"Will Dad be all right?"

"Yes, barring further complications. The healing process should take about three days, perhaps longer, then I will remove the tube."

"I want to see my husband," Anne said.

"By all means. As soon as they finish cleaning up." Dr. Crane put his arm around Anne. "But be prepared. He has a tube in his chest now, as well as the intravenous feeding tube."

"I can handle it."

"I know, Anne. But I also want you to know that right now Michael looks a lot worse than he is."

The door opened and a nurse came into the hallway. "The family can come in now."

They all crowded through the door, everybody except Jake. He would have gone if Emily had given any sign she wanted him to. But she hadn't. Not by glance or gesture or word.

Jake could picture them hovered around Michael, surveying the latest damage and willing it not to be so.

He'd wrecked them, then stayed to try to repair the damage and only succeeded in making it worse.

It was time to be moving on. Daniel was home. The Westmoreland family didn't need him anymore. Emily didn't need him.

Nor want him. And that was the thing that lacerated Jake's heart.

He could live with that. Maybe he needed that. Maybe it was just punishment for what he had done.

Tomorrow he would crawl back to Atlanta and lick his wounds. He would leave this family he'd been a part of for a short time, and they would band together in healing. Without him.

They would be better off without him. All of them. Even Emily.

Especially Emily.

* * *

"If there's nothing else I can do to help you, I'll be heading home to Atlanta tomorrow."

The voice was Jake's. Emily couldn't believe her ears. She stood in the downstairs hall, riveted. Eavesdropping.

It had been late when they came home from the hospital. Everybody except Anne, of course. They couldn't have blasted her away from Michael with dynamite.

They'd all said good-night and gone to their rooms, too tired to do or say more. The only reason Emily was downstairs was that she couldn't sleep.

Apparently neither could Jake.

Who else was in the den with him? Certainly not Hannah. In spite of her conciliatory remarks at the dinner table, she still merely tolerated him for the sake of the family.

It had to be Daniel. As if to confirm Emily's belief, her brother spoke.

"You've been more than generous already. I don't know how we'll ever thank you."

"No thanks necessary."

"You're welcome to stay as long as you like, Jake."

"Thanks, but I need to head on back."

Was he leaving now? Without saying goodbye? Emily was torn between racing back upstairs and hiding in her bed or storming into the den and confronting him.

Instead, she did neither. She stayed at her listening post.

"We'll see you at breakfast?"

"No, I'd like to get an early start."

"Take care, then."

It was Daniel's way of saying goodbye. Soon he'd be out in the hall, and Emily would be found out as the cowardly sister who didn't have enough spunk to speak her mind.

"You want to bet," she whispered, then she stormed the citadel.

"Em?" Daniel gave her a startled look, but it was nothing compared to the look on Jake's face. The look on his face made her want to cry—after she got finished being scared to death. Scared she was losing him. Scared she'd already lost him. "What brings you down here?"

"The same thing that brought you, big brother. Couldn't sleep."

"Join the club." Daniel's glance swung between Jake and Emily. He was nobody's fool. "I'm leaving it to the two of you. Night, all."

In the morning Emily would thank her brother. For everything. But right now she had other things on her mind. And she wasn't fixing to be bashful about saying them.

"So, you're leaving."

They stood facing each other like two gladiators. Emily was glorious in her rage, and under any other circumstances Jake would have kissed her thoroughly, then tossed her over his shoulder and carried her to the nearest bed. But these were spirit-sapping, dangerous circumstances. And from where he was standing, relief was not just over the horizon.

"You heard?"

"Yes. I was eavesdropping."

He caught himself before he laughed. No telling what that would do to an already volatile situation.

"I'm sorry, Em. I didn't mean for you to find out that way."

"How did you mean for me to find out? By carrier pigeon?"

"I was going to leave you a note."

"Isn't that a little impersonal, considering what we've been to each other?"

Her use of the past tense to describe their relationship slammed Jake in the gut. Harder than he'd expected.

"I didn't get a chance to tell you earlier, and I didn't want to wake you."

"I see."

That tone of voice. He'd never heard her use it. But then, what did he expect? She'd been through hell and back.

And he was the one who had put her there. He had to keep reminding himself of that. If he didn't he would give in to the almost overpowering urge to hold her. Hold her and not let go.

They stood staring at each other, a million unspoken words between them. And then she marched up to him, bold and dry-eyed, and hugged him. It was not the kind of hug you gave to a lover, but the kind you gave to somebody who was not quite friend but more than acquaintance. Brief. Impersonal. Not too tight.

"Goodbye, Jake."

That's all she said. Just goodbye. Was it the end, then? Or was she leaving the door open for him?

He couldn't bear to shut it. He couldn't stand to leave without some understanding between them.

"Em?" He put his hands on her cheeks and gently forced her to look at him. "I'll call you. Okay?"

For a moment she softened, but when she stepped out of his reach, there was nothing about her demeanor to encourage him.

"Whatever you wish," she said, then turned on her heel and marched out of the room. Back stiff. Head high.

Jake stood looking at the door long after she'd disappeared, then he went upstairs and packed his things. Afterward he lay in bed staring at the ceiling, trying not to think about anything except the long journey home.

Instead, he thought of Emily and all that he'd lost. A

woman like her came along only once in a lifetime. How had he let it all go so wrong?

He should have paid attention to his own rules. No involvement. He'd known better. Women and mountain climbing simply didn't mix. The breakup with Emily was inevitable. Even if Michael hadn't been caught in that avalanche, sooner or later something would have happened to drive them apart. If not on Everest, then on some other mountain.

Mountains were the most demanding mistresses in the world. They demanded total devotion, but most of all they demanded sacrifice.

This time the sacrifice had been too great. A very fine man lay in a coma, and an awesome woman lay in her bed down the hall, alone. Not asking for his company and not wanting it.

Jake kicked the twisted covers and looked at the bedside clock. It was after midnight.

He wasn't going to sleep tonight. He might as well just get out of bed and hit the road. If the turmoil of his own thoughts didn't keep him awake, coffee would. Besides, he enjoyed night driving.

Chapter Twenty-Three

July 14, 2001

I'm afraid to close my eyes. Afraid that if I'm not vigilant, something awful will happen to Michael.

When I first saw the chest tube they'd put in him this morning, I nearly burst out crying. Maybe I should have. Maybe outrage would plow its way through all that darkness that holds my husband captive. Maybe it would wake him up.

I must have dozed a moment ago, because when I jerked myself upright again I shouted, "Wake up!" The nurse came running and asked was anything wrong, and I told her, no, I'd just been talking to myself, that I didn't want to sleep after this morning's crisis.

She believed me, but I didn't believe myself. I was shouting at Michael. Mad. I wanted to shake him and say, "Get up out of that bed and come home where you belong."

I would never do such a thing, of course. How could I even think such a thing when he's lying there so helpless?

I've tried to focus on good things. Memories that make me smile. That's how I got through today's crisis.

After Dr. Crane said we could come back into this prison/room and I saw Michael, I started talking to the children about tomatoes. "Do you remember that time your father decided to have the earliest tomatoes in the neighborhood?" I asked them, and to their credit not a single one of my children looked at me as if I'd gone crazy.

Hannah said she remembered it vividly, but Daniel, who always seems to know exactly what a person needs, said, "Tell us about it, Mom."

I pulled a chair close to the bed and took Michael's hand, because I wanted him to hear it too. I was hoping he might even interrupt if I left out a vital part of the story, the way he sometimes does. Over the years we've developed a sort of Jerry Lewis/Dean Martin routine where it takes both of us to tell a story.

"He bought one of the early varieties of seeds. He could tell you the name. I can't."

I glanced at the bed to see if he were going to jump up and call out the name. He just lay there with his hair falling down into his eyes.

I brushed it back and continued my story.

"Remember how the seedlings sprouted in the windowsill and how he hovered over them like a mother hen until they were big enough to move outside? Still, they were much too young for fruit."

Hannah and Emily were smiling, and Daniel was chuckling outright. I'm so glad I could make my children smile. It's important to bring that kind of joy to others, especially your own children. I wonder why more people don't know that?

"'They'll bear tomatoes in no time,' I told him. 'A little sunshine is exactly what they need.'

"'I know what they need,' he said, then he hied himself off to the nearest grocery store and returned with four of the prettiest, ripest tomatoes I'd ever seen.

"He was whistling that snappy little tune he loves. I can't remember the name. What's it called, Michael?"

"Mom..." Hannah started to correct me, but Daniel gave her that look he has, and she didn't say anything else.

At that point I don't think I could have borne any more hard truths. Daniel understood. So did Emily. Hannah did, too, of course, but she's never been one to sit back and leave a situation alone if she thinks she can make it better.

"It's all right," I told her, in spite of the fact that nothing in my life will be all right again as long as Michael lies in this deep sleep.

"What's the rest of the story, Mom?" Emily asked, as if she hadn't heard it a million times, as if it were not the treasured story we trotted out at family gatherings for years afterward.

It was always good for a laugh, and God knows, all of us need laughter right now.

"Well," I said, "the next morning when I walked onto the verandah with my coffee, there were four of the biggest, ripest tomatoes I ever saw on that plant. 'Michael, come out here and see,' I yelled. 'It's a miracle.'"

"'Yep. It sure is,' he said.

"He wasn't surprised a bit, and that's what roused

my suspicions. I raced over there and bent down for a closer look. He'd tied the tomatoes on with twine.''

My children laughed as if they were hearing the story for the first time. Which was what I intended all along. To make them laugh. To make Michael want to join them.

We left those tomatoes tied to that vine for three days, and when Clark Gibbens saw them, he nearly died of jealousy. Our neighbor prides himself on being the best gardener in Vicksburg, and Michael was always trying to outdo him.

Every time he saw either of us after the tomato incident, he'd scratch his head and say, "I don't know how you did that." Neither Michael nor I ever told him the truth. To this good day he thinks Michael possesses some secret knowledge that he doesn't share.

I wonder what secrets Michael is keeping now. I wonder if he will tell me when he comes out of his coma.

If he comes out.

No, I can't let myself think like that. I won't. I will sit in this chair with my eyes wide open and remember another wonderful story.

A story to keep me vigilant. A story to make me smile.

Chapter Twenty-Four

Jake had his bags packed and was getting his car keys when his door creaked open. Emily stood silhouetted in the moonlight.

"Jake? May I come in?"

"You don't have to ask. Ever. Don't you know that, Em?"

She hovered near the doorway, arms wrapped around herself as if she were cold.

"I'm not sure. I'm not sure of anything anymore, Jake."

"These last few weeks have been hard. Maybe we expected too much of each other."

"And ourselves." She glanced at his suitcase. "You're leaving now?"

"I thought it best."

What did she want? Why was she here?

Jake tried to take his cue from her. He didn't want to

say or do anything else that would bring her pain, and so he kept his grip on his desire, as well as his suitcase.

The moon was impossibly bright. The space between them impossibly wide. They stared at each other across that vast gulf, filled with longing and regret, and neither of them knew how to build a bridge.

"I should be going, then," she said.

She turned away, and Jake knew with absolute certainty that if he let her go like that, he would never see her again.

"Em. Wait." He dropped his suitcase and crossed the room in three long strides. "I don't want you to go."

With his hands on her shoulders, he gently turned her around.

"Oh, Jake." She leaned into him, hugging him hard. "All I know is that I can't let you go with nothing more than a friendly hug. You…mean too much to me."

He rested his chin on her hair and closed his eyes. Once more he held the world, and he was so full he could hardly speak.

"You mean a lot to me, too, Em."

"I want us to say goodbye properly."

"Not goodbye. A kiss till I see you again."

"Yes. A kiss. And more. Please."

That was all the invitation Jake needed. He carried her to the bed and stripped away the simple white cotton nightshirt that separated them. Then with the moon shining through the window like a benediction, he explored her soft curves and sweet, secret places and rediscovered the terrains of the heart.

Coming to Jake in the middle of the night had been madness, but it was a madness Emily gladly embraced. They were not the kind of lovers who fanned the flames of passion gradually with sweet kisses and slow caresses. No lengthy foreplay for them.

They came together like two storm fronts. Bodies heaving. Blood boiling. Hearts hammering. Passion sizzling.

It was what Emily needed, what she wanted, this mind-bending forgetfulness, this banquet of the flesh, this heady erotic ride to oblivion.

Jake knew every inch of her, knew the magic places, knew the hot spots. Knew and ignited them all.

With him, Emily had discovered she was not a silent lover. Urgent murmurings tumbled from her, and she was hardly aware of speaking.

"Yes, yes, yes," she said when his mouth closed over a nipple.

She pressed her hands against the mounds of her breasts, offering them up to him like chalices. Her nipples were diamond hard and aching, aching for the touch of him. Only him.

Hot, liquid sensations flooded her, and she laced her hands through his hair, holding him close, not wanting him to leave, not ever wanting him to leave.

"I can't get enough of you," he murmured, and his passion-drugged voice was a deep, rich bell that resonated through her.

"I want...God, I'm so greedy. I want everything."

She arched high, and his fingers slid into her slick hot folds, searching, searing, satisfying.

"If I'm dreaming, don't wake me," she whispered, and then, quite suddenly, she was incapable of talk, incapable of thought. There was nothing at all except Jake's hands, his mouth, pressing, probing, and the fires that licked through her.

She cried out his name, and he lifted himself over her, caught her hips high and thrust home.

She owned the world. She was queen of the universe. Of all women, she was the most beloved.

A part of her stood back and marveled. How could it be? After all they'd been through, after the doubts and fears, the small separations, the unintentional hurts...how could their mating still be magic?

The magic engulfed her, and as he drove deep she tangled the sheet in her fists and gave an incoherent cry. She was burning, burning. Lust. Passion. Love. They were so intertwined she couldn't tell one from the other.

Nor did she want to. All she wanted was the deep, dark night and the never-ending magic of a man who defied mountains.

Forever. She wanted the night to go on forever.

Sweat slicked his back and dripped from his cheeks. She could taste his salt, and when he bent down to kiss her, her lips burned.

She didn't care. She wanted them to be bruised and puffy from his kisses. She wanted him to brand every inch of her body so that in the morning when she awoke and he was gone, at least she'd have that. Small reminders of him. A rawness that would distract her from the pain in her heart.

Emily lay curved against him, her skin rosy with the flush of love and the first pink rays of dawn. How was he ever going to leave her?

Quickly. Without goodbyes.

They'd said their goodbyes last night. Without words. With bodies and souls and hearts united in a marathon of lust and love.

He eased back the covers. Emily stirred, stretched, yawned. Then reached to the other side of the bed and found it empty.

"Jake?" She sat up, pulling the sheet with her.

"I didn't want to wake you, Emily."

"Why?"

"I wanted to be gone before you woke up."

"You were going to leave without saying anything?"

He knelt on the bed and cupped her face. "We said everything we needed to say. Last night. Right here in this bed."

"But, Jake—"

He put his fingers over her mouth, rubbed her full lower lip lightly. Then unable to resist, he bent to kiss her. Softly. Tenderly.

"What else is there to say, Em?"

"Well…"

She pushed her hair back from her face, and the sheet slid to her waist. Her breasts were reddened from his beard stubble. Her nipples, hot hard points.

He couldn't take his eyes off her. Couldn't stop his mouth from tasting her.

She tangled her hands in his hair, pulled him close. Held him there, moaning. Both of them incoherent with desire and pain.

"This," she whispered. "There's always this." She kicked the sheet aside and pulled him down to her. "One more time…before you go."

How could he deny her? How could he deny himself?

When he entered her, time and place ceased to exist. Nothing mattered except the two of them, and desire so intense it stole reason.

Together they created a magic that swept them out to sea, a sea of swirling passion and shimmering pleasures. They rode the waves, crested slowly, ever so slowly, until at last they crashed onto the hard and sandy shore.

The light coming over the windowsill had changed from

pink to a blinding gold. Tomorrow had finally come. Reality could no longer be denied.

"I have to go, Em."

"I know." She shoved at the tangled covers. "I'll get dressed and see you off."

"No. I want you to stay here."

"Why?"

"I want to remember you this way. Flushed from our lovemaking. The sheets tangled around you."

She reached for another pillow and propped herself up.

"You'll call me?"

"Yes."

"And I'll call you."

"Good. I want you to."

"I'll let you know what's happening with Dad."

The room was suddenly electric with tension.

"Yes, I'll want to know."

What else was there to say? Jake grabbed his pants and headed for the bathroom. When he came back Emily was still propped on the pillows. She watched silently while he dressed, then gathered his belongings.

He stood at the edge of the bed looking down at her. She was so beautiful she made his heart ache. He wanted to always remember her this way, dark hair fanned across the pillows, skin and eyes glowing.

"Jake…"

He bent swiftly and kissed her. "Till we meet again, Em," he whispered, and then he was striding out the door. He didn't stop until he got outside.

Don't look back, he told himself, and got in his car. Then he turned the key in the ignition and drove away from Belle Rose, away from the place where for a short while he'd known magic.

* * *

Emily stared at the closed door, dry-eyed and hurting. She should get up and go to her room. What if Hannah came looking for her? Or Daniel? What if her mother called and needed her?

Jake is gone. We didn't even make plans to see each other again.

She closed her eyes against the pain that engulfed her, and when she opened them again, Hannah was standing in the doorway, hands on her hips.

"I went to your room, but you weren't there. I figured I'd find you here."

"You make it sound like an accusation."

"It's not an accusation, merely an observation. Obviously you're old enough to make your own decisions in matters of the heart."

Emily didn't know what to say to her sister, so she said nothing.

"It *is* a matter of the heart, isn't it, Em?"

"Yes."

It was Hannah's turn to remain silent. She went to the window and threw the curtains wide open.

"I like sunshine," she said, then turning to Emily, she added, "Be careful that you don't let him break it."

"He's not that kind."

"Under ordinary circumstances, maybe not. But these are extraordinary circumstances."

How well she knew. Hadn't the mere mention of her father's accident spread a chill she'd felt all the way to her bones?

Her face must have shown her dismay, for Hannah sat on the edge of the bed and put an arm around her.

"I'm sorry, kid. I wish things were different."

Sympathy always made Emily cry, but she'd be darned if she was going to sit in bed and wail like a baby.

Jake was only going to Atlanta. She'd have to keep telling herself that.

"What time is it?" she asked.

"Eleven."

"Good grief. I have to get dressed. I have to get to the hospital."

"Daniel left early this morning. I'm going right after lunch."

"But I—"

"You don't have to do it all now, Em. Your family is here. Remember that."

Suddenly Emily realized how tired she was. And how very lucky she was. She wrapped her arms around her sister.

"Oh, God, Hannah. I'm so glad you're home."

Chapter Twenty-Five

July 28, 2001

This hospital room is a prison, and if I keep staying here day in and day out, I'm going to go stark raving crazy. I want to go home. I want to sleep in my own bed and wake up with sun coming through my window. I want to have breakfast on the porch and watch the cardinals playing in the fountain. I want to smell the gardenias.

Are they still in bloom? I don't even know what's blooming in my own garden. I have to bite my tongue to keep from yelling at Michael, "WAKE UP! CAN'T YOU SEE WHAT THIS IS DOING TO US? TO ME?"

I don't even want to call him "darling" anymore. He doesn't call me pet names. He doesn't call me at all.

Is this normal? This rage?

Maybe I should talk to somebody about it. A professional. This is not something I can share with my children, even Daniel who is trained to know about such things. They're worried enough about their father. They don't need to worry about me, too, a perfectly healthy woman who can walk and talk and bathe herself.

That's another thing. I won't let anybody bathe Michael except me. He's such a private man. Having a stranger lift up the sheets to wash him would be the ultimate indignity.

I don't even let Daniel do it.

He left this morning, going back to Atlanta. Undaunted, it seems, by the lack of progress here. We have to have faith, Mom, he told me when he came to say goodbye. And then he prayed the most beautiful prayer. I wish I could remember all of it. Part of it went like this: "God, we place your child Michael in your loving arms and ask that you keep him safe from harm until he's ready to come back to us."

Daniel's faith never wavers. I wish I could say the same for myself. Last night when I tried to ask for healing, I found myself, instead, hurling accusations. How could a benevolent God let this bad thing happen to Michael, of all people? He's a good man, a kind, generous man who loves his wife and adores his children. He's a good citizen who votes and pays his taxes and gives to charity.

Why did he get caught in an avalanche, instead of somebody who goes around shooting up public restaurants and breaking into houses?

I don't know. I just don't know anything anymore.

Except that I must go back to Belle Rose, at least for a little while. I need to feel my china teacup in my hand. I need to smell the coffee perking each morning. I need to stand on the balcony and look down at the curve where the Mississippi meets the Yazoo and feel that I'm part of something real.

I'm beginning not to feel real anymore. I'm beginning to lose myself in this impersonal place.

Besides, if I don't get my life back to some semblance of normal, Emily and Hannah will feel obligated to keep staying at Belle Rose. I won't let them do that. Hannah has another assignment—out in Yellowstone, I think she said—and Emily needs to be back in Tallahatchie River Bottom among the trees and woodland flowers and animals so she can heal.

She's broken. She tries to hide it, but I can see through her. She and Jake haven't seen each other in two weeks.

Oh, they've talked. Briefly. Not every day the way Michael and I did when we first met. That's what lovers do. They can't bear not to hear the sound of their beloved's voice, even for one day. Sometimes the talk is as inconsequential as the weather, but still, you feel the connection. The heart tug. The wonderful yearning. And the beautiful sense of promise.

Here's a man who loves me, you say to yourself when that phone call comes. Here's a man who can't wait until he sees me again. He can't wait another minute before telling me how much he wants to see me. How much he wants me.

That's the way it was with Michael and me.

Who knows about Jake and Emily? Maybe I'm wrong. Maybe I only saw what I wanted to the day they met, but I would swear I saw true love.

Yesterday I said to Emily, "Love is easy when everything's going smoothly. The real test comes when bad things happen, when there's sickness or death or financial disaster. Even a string of small day-to-day disappointments and irksome circumstances can put a strain on a relationship."

"But that didn't happen to you and Dad, did it?" she asked me.

"Are you kidding? There was a time when Michael and I almost broke up."

"I can't believe it."

"Believe it," I told her. "Every relationship has problems. If it doesn't then something is wrong. Somebody's not telling the truth."

It amazes me that even my own child thinks love is some kind of magic potion that banishes all problems. It's not. I said to my daughter that there will always be little hurts and misunderstandings in a relationship. The real trick is not in overcoming them, but in knowing if the relationship itself is real.

There's so much more I need to tell Emily, to tell all my children. I guess if I had to sum up true love in one sentence, I would say it creates an environment where a person can live fully and with passion, not just of the body but of the soul and the spirit.

Michael and I have always had that. I guess we're lucky. I've seen so many people chained together in marriages that crush the spirit and kill the soul. Why they stay is beyond me.

I refuse to live in a narrow, boxed-in way. Even now, with Michael unable to take me in his arms and tell me he loves me, I still feel cherished. I still wouldn't trade places with anybody else. With anybody whose husband is present in body and mind but not spirit, a man who lacks that essential quality—the ability to live passionately. No, more than just the ability. The hunger.

The nurse will be coming soon to turn Michael.

They've put lamb's wool underneath him to protect his skin.

"Feel how soft it is, Michael," I told him last night as I cuddled beside him with my hand on his chest and my head on his shoulder. (They removed the chest tube last week, thank God.) He didn't say anything, and I simply lay there listening to the beat of his heart.

Did he feel mine, I wonder? Did the pulsing of my blood rouse something buried deep in him? Memories? Desire? Anger?

I wish he'd get mad. Mad about the hyperalimentation line (a fancier thing than the old feeding tube) and the daily parade of nurses with crepe-soled shoes. Mad about sleeping the summer away, missing so much of his life.

I can't write any more about anger. My hand is starting to shake.

Tomorrow I'm going back to Belle Rose. At least for lunch. Maybe I'll even spend the night. I think it would do us both good.

Maybe Michael can't come back because my expectations are too heavy for him. I expect him to wake up whole, all his memories intact, all his desires, his humor, his love of life.

Maybe when he wakes up, he'll be a different Michael. Reduced, somehow. Memories stripped away. Humor forgotten. Desire gone forever.

I won't think about that right now. I'll think about going home and being a mother. Hannah needs me to tell her to take that assignment out West. Emily needs me to send her back to her animals. She needs my counsel.

I'm going to give her some diary pages to read. From

that time I almost lost Michael. Or, as he said, he almost lost me.

I'll have to remind him of that. I'll have to tell him he'd better not even think of staying in that coma. "You'd better wake up, Michael," I'll say, "because I don't intend to lose you again."

Chapter Twenty-Six

These days, every time the phone rang Emily jumped out of her skin, expecting it to be either the hospital with bad news or Jake with good. She didn't know exactly what she expected from Jake. Something along the lines of, *I can't stand another day without you, Em. I'm coming over to see you.* Or, *Why don't you hop on a plane and fly in for the weekend, Em? I've been doing some thinking, and I've come to the conclusion that nothing can keep us apart.*

None of these conversations ever take place, of course. That was why Emily snaps at Hannah over the least little thing. Like not putting the top back on the peanut-butter jar. As if it matters. As if a lifetime of sisterhood boils down to nothing more than a jar of dried-out peanut butter.

All these thoughts tumbled through Emily's mind as she tore lettuce for salads. Anne was coming home for lunch today. Finally. And if Hannah and Emily could talk some sense into her, she'd stay the night.

The phone cut into her reverie.

"I'll get it!" she yelled, and then breathless, Emily picked up the receiver. "Hello?"

"Emily. It's Jake."

Emily hooked a bentwood bar stool with her toe and dragged it over so she could get comfortable, then settled in for a long conversation. She hoped.

"How are things in Atlanta?"

That was what she asked. A foolish question whose answer didn't matter a flip. What she really wanted to know was this: when are you coming to Mississippi?

"Fine," he said. "How are you, Emily?"

Was that a real question, or was Jake merely being polite? How she was, was awful. She felt like a cracked china plate that had been patched together with glue that might not hold her through the next meal. And certainly wouldn't hold her through a dishwashing cycle.

"Good," she told him. "I'm hanging in there."

God, she hated trite expressions. And now she'd reduced herself to one.

"Any change in Michael?"

"No."

What else was there to say? I hope he'll wake up soon? *Everybody* hoped that. Even Jake. Especially Jake.

"I'm sorry, Em."

The sudden silence between them was wide and deep. Emily twisted the phone cord around her finger, waiting for it to end.

"Let me know if there's anything I can do."

If she responded to that truthfully she would say, *You can come and hold my hand till it's all over.* The thing was, nobody knew when it would all be over. Nor how it would end.

"Sure," she said.

And then he said, "Goodbye, I'll be seeing you," and she sat on the bar stool with the receiver in her hand listening to the sound of an electronic voice saying, "If you wish to make a call, please hang up and dial again."

"I can guess who that was."

Hannah was standing in the doorway with her hands on her hips.

"Don't," Emily said.

She spoke more sharply than she'd meant to, and Hannah didn't say anything. She just went to the cabinet, got out a knife and started chopping vegetables. Hard.

Emily started making tea, slamming the teapot on the burner, banging the cabinet door open, throwing ice cubes into the glasses...feeling perfectly justified. Two could play the same game.

The silent battle raged through the kitchen, and all of a sudden Emily felt ridiculous. And small.

Hannah was her sister. Her best friend. She remembered the day she'd seen a red feather drift to the ground, and how she'd raced to tell Hannah, then together they waited under the spreading canopy of the oak tree in the front yard, hoping to catch a cardinal in the act of shedding another feather. For good luck, they'd told each other. And so Hannah could have a feather to stick in her baseball cap, too.

Emily had kept that feather for five years, believing for at least three of them that it really *did* bring good luck. Then one day it had drifted away on a breeze while she was rounding third base, making for home plate in the baseball game that had won a championship for her junior-high school.

Nobody ever found it. That was the funny thing. Later Hannah swore she'd seen it fly all the way up to the heavens, fly so high it had gone beyond the treetops directly into the path of the sun.

Emily set the teapot up to steep. Carefully this time.

"Remember that cardinal's feather, Hannah?"

"Yeah."

"I wonder whatever happened to it."

"Jimmy Buskirk put it in his pocket."

"You never told me. Why didn't you tell me that?"

"You'd have bloodied his nose. Besides, didn't you like the other version better?"

"Yes... Hannah, I'm glad you're my sister."

"Me, too, kid. But I'm your *older* sister..."

"That doesn't mean you know everything, especially what's best for me."

"I'm not saying I know what's best for you, Emily, but in this case I can certainly see things that you can't or won't see."

"Such as?"

"A man who is interested in a woman will find a way to be with her, no matter what."

"Good Lord, Hannah. I can't believe you. You're beginning to sound like Grandmother Beaufort."

"As a matter of fact, she did say that. And in this case it's painfully obvious."

Emily was about to take umbrage again. She could feel it in her face. Her nose always swelled and turned red when she got mad.

Any minute now their mother would be walking through the door, and she wasn't about to be caught in a tussle of words with Hannah. Furthermore, she knew her sister never held her tongue under any circumstances, so why should she expect her to start now?

"Maybe you're right," Emily said.

Hannah gave her this squinty-eyed, suspicious look, then burst out laughing.

"All right, Em. I'll let you play possum this time. But don't expect me to keep my mouth shut much longer."

"That would be a first."

"Have you tried that stinger on Jake? Maybe that's what he needs to get his butt in gear. That is, if you want him to get it in gear… Do you, Em?"

There was the heart of the matter.

Had they wounded each other too deeply? Could they ever overcome their circumstances? Would they ever be able to come together without guilt?

"I don't know," she said.

All she knew was that she wished she had a red feather…and that it really did bring luck.

After a lunch that lasted well into the afternoon, Anne decided quite suddenly to spend the night at Belle Rose. Much to the delight of her daughters. Of course, most of the credit belonged to Hannah, who said she was going to the hospital that night regardless of what Anne decided about staying home, and knowing her oldest daughter as she did, Anne acquiesced.

Now Emily and her mother were sitting on the love seat in Anne's suite, eating popcorn from a blue bowl, the way they'd done on so many evenings. It felt good. Emily was the first to admit it. Out loud.

"This is great, Mom. It feels almost like old times."

"It does, doesn't it."

"I'm glad you decided to stay."

"So am I. I've been thinking…Em, how would you feel if I stopped staying at the hospital every night?"

"Maybe it's time you did, Mom. For the sake of your health, if nothing else."

"Oh, I don't mean I wouldn't still spend most of my time there. I was thinking…I could go every morning and help Michael with his bath, then come home for lunch and go back midafternoon. Take a book from the library to read to him, take fresh flowers from the garden. Bake bread and let him smell the fresh yeasty scent. That sort of thing.''

''Sounds good.''

''Sometimes I wouldn't come home, of course. I need to be able to reach out and touch him at night. I...need to sleep with him, Em.''

Emily thought of a book she'd read, *When Elephants Weep*. She thought of how some animals mate for life and will stay for days at the side of a fallen mate, even after the body has grown cold.

Then she was horrified that she'd thought of her father as nothing more than a body growing cold.

''You do whatever you need to, Mom. I'll be here to help you.''

''No. I want you to go home, Emily.''

''I *do* need to get back to my work. As long as Hannah's here...''

''I want her to leave, too. I want her to take that assignment.''

''And leave you alone?''

''Yes.'' Anne caught her hands. ''Emily, we don't know how long this is going to go on. I won't have my children putting their lives on hold. This is my problem...and Michael's. He's my husband.''

''You know we're not going to abandon you and Dad.''

''It's not abandonment, Emily. It's living. Besides, you have another problem that needs your full attention.''

''Jake?''

''Yes.''

''I'm not so sure about that. I don't know how to interpret his silences. At this point I don't even understand my own feelings toward him.''

"Maybe this will help you."

Anne reached into her desk and handed Emily a sheaf of yellowed pages from her diary. "Not that I claim to be an expert. Not by any stretch of the imagination. But sometimes the words and deeds of those who have gone before us can act as a beacon to light our path."

Chapter Twenty-Seven

December 1, 1966

I am so mad I don't know what to do. Michael left for Italy to film in the Dolomites two weeks ago, and the only word I've had from him has been from Sam, the cameraman. He called today to say that Michael had met with a little accident in the mountains. Of course, I nearly died when he said that. I think I screamed, "Is he dead?" And Sam told me, "No, just banged up, fell and broke his collarbone, but it could just as well have been his neck."

Well, I certainly didn't need that information. What did the idiot think I thought about every minute while Michael was on that mountain? Or any mountain, for that matter.

Disaster. That's what.

And now it has struck.

"Where is he?" I asked Sam. "I'll be right there."

And then this Sam character said the thing that changed me all of sudden from heartsick and scared to mad as an old wet hen. He said, "Michael doesn't want to see you. He asked me to tell you not to come. Said it would be better this way."

"Better what way?" I asked Sam, but he hemmed and hawed and finally said, "None of this is my business. I just made the call, that's all."

I would have felt sorry for the poor man if I hadn't been feeling so sorry for myself. What I was thinking is, all these months of loving a man have come to this: me on one continent and Michael on another, and him hurt and saying don't come.

Well, if he thinks I'm going to sit still and let the love of a lifetime slip through my fingers, he's got another think coming, as Mother always says. I know she wouldn't approve, but the minute he gets back to the States, I'm going to have a showdown with him. He can't simply vanish from my life without a word.

December 2, 1966

Word came today. In the form of a letter. A letter I wished I'd never received. "My beloved," Michael wrote. "By some miracle I only broke my collarbone, but I shudder to think how easily it could have been my neck. And then you'd be saddled with a cripple. I won't do that to you. The risks of my profession are too great. I can't ask you to share them."

He told me those horrible things, then signed the letter, "All my love, Michael."

Does he really think I'm a hothouse flower who has to be protected? Shielded from painful truths?

How dare he make this decision without discussing it with me? How dare he send me what amounts to a Dear Jane letter without giving me a chance to say how I feel about the whole matter?

My first instinct is to say all those things to him in person. And yet...he knows me. He knows I'm made of sterner stuff. He knows I'm a constant woman, not a will-o'-the-wisp.

Plus, he's the most stubborn man on two continents. Perhaps the world. He's made up his mind to disappear from my life, and no amount of reasoning on my part will change that.

I never thought I'd stoop to games. With him or anybody else. But circumstances warrant drastic measures, and I know just the measure to take. Perhaps it won't work, especially on a man like Michael, a man clever enough to see through the whole scheme, and yet, I can't sit back and do nothing. I won't.

Tonight I'm calling Herman Richmond and asking him to take me to dinner. And I'll make darned sure Michael knows.

Mother would be so proud of me.

December 10, 1966

My plan was a roaring success, "roaring" being the operative word. I suspected Michael would react when he discovered my old flame was squiring me around town, but I never suspected he would descend on us like Hannibal storming the Alps. I never expected him to literally pluck me out of my seat at the Met, and then drag me off like a caveman.

What he did was tap Herman on the shoulder and

say, "Excuse me, she's mine." Then he scooped me out of my seat and carried me off.

Heads turned. A few people applauded. Some called out encouragement. It's good to know that even in a city as jaded as Manhattan, romance is still alive and well.

Michael never paused to wonder why Herman gave up without a fight, and of course, I'll never tell him. Herman was in on the scheme from the beginning. And wholeheartedly approved. He loves drama.

I wouldn't have done it otherwise. Claiming a few scruples takes away the stench of mendacity. (I love that word. Have ever since I saw *Cat on a Hot Tin Roof*.)

We spent the rest of the evening making up. Mmm. YUMMY!

Michael's sleeping now. Deeply, the way he always does. Right before he fell asleep he said to me, "I can't believe how close I came to losing you." I kissed him and said, "Go to sleep now, darling. You didn't lose me. You never will."

I love the way he looks stretched out on the bed so that he takes up most of the space the way a tall, well-built man does. I love that look of peace on his face after we've made love. And I love knowing I put it there.

Such a dear face. What would I have done if my scheme hadn't worked? How would I ever live without him?

I don't even want to think about it.

Instead, I'll think about something wonderful. The future. My graduation. The concert tour.

Michael is taking me dancing to celebrate. There is no one in the world I'd rather celebrate with than my beloved Michael.

Chapter Twenty-Eight

The thing that stood out above all else for Emily was her mother's deep love for Michael Westmoreland. She folded the diary pages and slipped them into her desk drawer. Then she went into the bathroom and blew her nose on a strip of toilet tissue. She never had the real thing when she needed it.

Gwendolyn cocked her head and looked up at Emily as if to say, *What's wrong?*

"It's all right, sweetcakes." She bent to pet the skunk. "Don't worry your pretty little head over it."

She and Gwendolyn had been back in the woods for almost a week, and it was only now that Emily had decided to read her mother's diary. She knew what had prompted her decision, of course.

Jake's phone call last night.

"How's Michael?"

He'd asked that first thing, as he always did, and when

Emily said, "The same," they both fell into one of those long silences that was becoming the rule rather than the exception for them.

"Romance is like bread," Grandmother Beaufort was fond of saying. "If it's left too long without attention, it grows stale."

For the first time in her life, Emily saw the logic in her grandmother's oft-repeated bit of advice.

"Good grief, Gwendolyn," she told her skunk. "I'm turning into my grandmother."

Hannah would get a kick out of that. Before they'd both left Belle Rose, she had come into Emily's room for a late-night talk.

"The thing that bothers me," Hannah had told her sister, "is that you're in danger of losing yourself."

She'd been talking about Emily's relationship with Jake, though by tacit agreement, neither of them spoke his name. It was best, considering the circumstances.

Though Hannah had made the proper noises toward Jake, it had been obvious to everybody that she still held him in some ways accountable for Michael's coma.

Emily didn't. Not anymore. And maybe she never had. Maybe the shock of seeing her father helpless had skewed her thinking processes, turned everything upside down and inside out so that even she couldn't recognize the truth.

Well, she simply couldn't think about it anymore. None of it.

"Let's go for a walk, Gwendolyn." The skunk needed no urging, but trailed along behind Emily as eagerly as a well-trained dog.

"Who knows? Maybe we'll find a nice little boy skunk for you, and you'll fall in love and get married and have lots of little skunk babies and live happily ever after."

That was when Emily started to cry. Crumpled onto a

bed of moss, the same one where she and Jake had whiled away a beautiful afternoon with such passion and joy, she cried for everything that was painful and impossible in a world somehow gone awry.

Or had it always been that way? Had she merely been fooling herself into thinking there was such a thing as finding the love of your life and having everything work out all right? Maybe that sort of thing really didn't happen—except for a lucky few.

Her parents just got lucky. That was it.

They'd found each other against all odds, and it was foolish of Emily to be thinking that lightning could strike twice in the same family. Maybe God rationed out luck the way he did thunderstorms, and Anne and Michael got all the Westmorelands' share.

She pulled her shirttail out of her shorts and wiped her eyes with the hem.

"I'm going to have to start carrying tissues," she told Gwendolyn.

She despised being that kind of woman. The kind prone to tears at the drop of a hat. She was going to have to get a grip. Buck up. Regain her equilibrium. Reclaim her sass.

Maybe Hannah had been right.

Emily stood up and dusted off the seat of her pants.

"Do you see a cute little bushy-tailed male around here, Gwendolyn? No? Well, look on the bright side. At least we have each other."

She'd started out of the forest glade when the feather floated down and landed right at her feet. A cardinal's feather. Bright as a bleeding heart.

Emily started to pass by it. It was Gwendolyn who stopped to sniff, Gwendolyn who stubbornly refused to leave the spot.

"Well, all right, if you insist." Emily bent down and

scooped up the feather. "But I have to tell you, Gwendolyn, I don't believe in that sort of magic anymore."

Nonetheless she tucked the feather behind her ear, and the odd thing was, she really did feel better. As if the red feather had magical powers.

By the time she came in sight of her cottage, she was beginning to feel more like herself. She even started to hum.

And that was when she saw him. Her love. Standing on the front porch shading his eyes against the sun and smiling.

She didn't say anything, mainly because she didn't know what to say. She was afraid of giving away her heart when all the time he'd come to say goodbye.

But he wouldn't be smiling if he'd come to do that, would he? He wouldn't have driven all the way from Atlanta to tell her something he could say over the telephone, would he?

The minute Jake saw Emily, he knew he'd been right to come—and a fool for not coming sooner.

"Where'd you get the hair ornament?" he asked.

"I found it in the woods. Actually, Gwendolyn found it."

"Did you find anything else?"

"Just memories."

Something inside Jake unfolded, some part of him that had been holding its breath for so long it had almost forgotten how to breathe.

Emily was now standing in front of him, just standing there with the feather in her hair and a hopeful smile on her face. It was all the invitation he needed. He walked right up to her and took her into his arms as if they'd never been apart, as if there was nothing between them except good times and good memories.

He cupped her face, tipping it up so he could study it, every beloved detail, the curve of her cheek, the shape of her lips, the deep green of her eyes.

"I've missed you," he said.

"So have I...missed you." She sighed, then leaned her forehead against his chest so that her voice was muffled. "Very, very much."

"I shouldn't have stayed away so long."

"You're here now."

"For a little while."

She lifted her head and looked at him, puzzled now, and uncertain. He silently cursed his choice of words.

"I didn't mean that the way it sounded," he said. "I'm taking clients to Dapsang next week. That's all I meant."

He didn't have to explain. The daughter of a climber, she knew where and what it was, the world's second-highest mountain, sometimes called K2, located in the Karakoram Range of the Himalayas.

"Oh...well, then..."

"Emily, I came because I couldn't *not* come."

His hands were still on her face, and it felt so good he didn't want to leave that spot. He didn't want to go inside where they would sit in chairs that somehow grounded them to the real world. Outside with the song of birds surrounding them and the sun shining down warm and golden, they were in a place divorced from reality, a place where all things were possible. Even an impossible love.

"I know...I know."

"I've thought of you every day, and no matter how hard I tried to rationalize staying away, I just couldn't."

"I'm glad you couldn't. If you hadn't come here, I

would have come there. In spite of Grandmother Beaufort's rules.''

He laughed for the sheer joy of it. One of the things he'd always admired most about Emily was her honesty. Rare, he believed. Rare and precious.

''And what rules would those be?''

''How young ladies of class comport themselves in the presence of the male species.''

''You, of course, broke every rule—and still do.''

''At every opportunity.''

''You don't know what a relief that is to me, Miss Emily.''

She was smiling in the way she had when he first knew her, a full-bodied, open smile that invited a person to come closer, to sit down and relax because there would be no judgment coming from her.

To think he'd almost lost it, all of it. And now, as much as he wanted to throw her over his shoulder and march into her house and make love with her until they were both sweating and sated, he also wanted to give her something more. Quiet dinners where the two of them held hands and gazed at each other across the table. Evenings at the movies where they would sit side by side with one bag of popcorn, both dipping their hands in at the same time so their fingers would touch, buttery slick. Hot chocolate by the firelight with Emily in the pink bathrobe that made her feel like a cuddly kitten and Jake bending over her massaging her feet. Kissing her toes. And wanting more. That was what he wanted. And if that made him a man longing to join the ranks of the domesticated, then so be it.

He would tell Emily all of that. And more.

But not now. First they would walk in the woods, then have a quiet dinner, and then…paradise. Soul-restoring paradise. For one whole week.

Afterward he would leave for Dapsang, get that climb behind him, and maybe, just maybe, Michael would be out of the coma when Jake returned.

Then he would tell Emily everything that was in his heart.

Emily was standing there in the sunshine happy but wondering what was coming next when Jake said, "What do you say we take Gwendolyn on another walk, Em?"

"Yes," she said, and that was how simple it was. This coming back together after an estrangement that seemed to have gone on forever.

Jake reached for her hand, and it felt just right to walk that way with him, lightly connected, no pressure, no questions, nothing except the two of them trailed by a very happy skunk.

Oh, Gwendolyn was a sight, swishing her tail in ecstasy because Jake was back.

That was how Emily felt. Like swishing. If she'd had a tail she would, and she just might, anyhow.

"I have a feeling this is going to be a good day," Jake said.

"Yes."

"For finding Gwendolyn a companion."

"Oh?" She hadn't been thinking of Gwendolyn at all, but of the two of them as perfect together as a matched set of anything you could name. Horses, maybe. Thoroughbreds. The kind you might see galloping over the greenest grass imaginable somewhere in Kentucky.

"See how she's prancing. Almost like flirting."

"Yes, but I think she's flirting with you."

Jake laughed, and oh, it was music to Emily's ears. Somehow all the troubles they'd gone through during the past few weeks shrank to their proper size. Instead of dominating their lives, the coma and all the events surrounding it became something that could be contained in one part of the mind without tainting everything else.

For weeks Emily had been wrestling with feelings of anger at both herself and Jake. They'd boiled inside her like a volcano getting ready to explode. She'd burned with the need to spew them out, to get rid of them no matter who got hurt.

She'd been torn apart by her conflicting needs to push him away and to grab hold of him and not let go.

Now, walking beside him in the quiet woods far away from a brooding mountaintop in the Himalayas and a lonely hospital bed in Vicksburg, she felt only a sense of rightness, of having come through a storm on a leaky raft and discovering to her amazement that she hadn't lost a single one of her possessions.

She didn't even feel any need to talk to him about what had gone on before.

"Sometimes we can analyze a situation to death, Em," her father used to tell her.

Oh, he was extremely wise. And she missed him so.

And yet…life goes on.

That was what she was thinking, life goes on, when all of a sudden Jake squeezed her hand and nodded in the direction of the stream, which meandered through the woods. There on its sloping, grassy bank strolled a magnificent male creature, a heartthrob skunk if ever there was one.

Gwendolyn had seen him, too. She hid herself behind Jake's legs and peered around, curious at first, and then fascinated. Her tail waved like a banner, and her lively little face twitched.

"I think she's shy," Jake whispered.

"All she needs is a mother's advice," Emily whispered

back, then quietly she knelt beside her most difficult rescue-and-rehabilitation challenge. "Go on, Gwendolyn. I think he likes you as much as you like him."

She gave Gwendolyn a little push in the right direction, but the skunk went only two feet, then stood rooted to the spot, torn between a comfortable life she knew and the exciting but possibly scary one she did not.

The male skunk had spotted her, but wary of humans, he'd stopped beside a bush big enough to provide instant shelter in case he needed it.

Jake squatted beside Emily and gave Gwendolyn a little nudge. "It's all up to you, girl."

"Isn't it always?"

"We'll discuss that later, Miss Em."

She loved it when Jake called her that. He called her other pet names, too, and she loved them all.

Suddenly she was tired of being matchmaker to a skunk. What she wanted was a bit of matching for herself. Or was that mating? The thought of it made her blush, and Jake didn't pretend not to notice.

He lifted an eyebrow, then reached out and traced her lips with the tip of his finger. Ever so softly.

Emily sighed, her mission completely forgotten. She and Jake yearned toward each other and met somewhere in the middle, their mouths open and hungry, their eyes wide open, studying each other, memorizing each other, loving each other.

Oh, it had to be love, didn't it? Nothing else could feel this perfect.

Jake wrapped his arms around her, pulling her close, and there was nothing else in the world except the two of them kissing. Kissing as if their lives depended on it.

"Let's go to bed," Jake said.

And she said, "Oh, yes. Please."

When he took her hand and pulled her to her feet, she noticed that Gwendolyn was gone.

"Where's Gwendolyn?"

Jake nodded in the direction of the stream, and when Emily looked, all she saw was two bushy waving tails, disappearing into the deep woods.

"Looks like they have the same idea," Jake said.

"So it seems."

"Let's see him top this."

Jake scooped her into his arms and raced toward the cabin laughing. And Emily owned the world.

Chapter Twenty-Nine

How can you describe heaven?

That was what Emily was thinking as she lay on her bed with Jake finally inside her. At long last. Back where he belonged. Where they both belonged.

"Stay," she whispered. "Don't move."

And then she wrapped her arms and legs around him and held him so close they felt like one person with one heart and one soul and one body suspended in this beautiful space, which could only be called home.

She remembered what her father used to say about it. *Home is not a place, it's a person, the one person in the world who feels exactly right to us and who makes us feel exactly right about ourselves.*

Emily and her siblings would be sitting on the rug around Michael's feet after he'd returned from one of his high-altitude filming expeditions, and she'd wondered what he meant by that.

Now she knew.

She was lying on top of a quilt with the sunshine pouring through the windows while she held the one person in the world she could call *home*. The place inside her that always quivered when something wasn't right, was at peace. And filled with exultation. Yes, that was the word for it. She wasn't merely happy inside and out, she was in a state of bliss that could only be called exultation.

Weaving her hands through Jake's hair, she held him close and whispered, "I love you, Jake. So very, very much."

And though he didn't say it back, she knew, anyhow. She knew. Love was in his eyes and in the way he touched her cheek, the way he kissed her. With a tenderness and passion that filled her heart.

Love was in the way he held on to her as if he would never let her go, and in the way he caressed her, his fingers skimming lightly over her skin, sending shivers of pleasure that went all the way to her soul.

"Ahh," she said, for how could she keep quiet when he was showing her paradise over and over again. And then quite suddenly she was screaming, "Yes, yes, yes!" for in that quicksilver way that thrilled her to the bone, Jake had gone from exquisitely tender to extraordinarily passionate, and she was a comet streaking across the sky, falling, falling in a trail of fire only to be reborn and rocketing toward the heavens once more.

Chapter Thirty

August 15, 2001

Last night I dreamed Michael and I were on a beach in Honolulu and he was bending over me, removing the top of my swimsuit and saying, "You are the most exquisite creature," in that wonderfully tender and intimate way he has. The way that makes me melt. Every time. Not just occasionally, but every single time.

And I was wondering in my dream how I got to be so lucky to find a man like him, a once-in-a-lifetime man I would love forever. One who would love me right back. Even when I'm gray and my belly is sagging and my legs look like cottage cheese. Even when I lose my teeth.

Then I woke up crying, and I realized I'd been crying all along, and that now I can't escape the truth even in my dreams. Michael's not here anymore. Not just here in Belle Rose in my bed, but here, period. Even though

I see his skin growing paler by the day and his eyelashes resting on his cheeks and his feet getting dry and cracked in spite of my efforts with lotion, he's still not here.

I was so furious I got out of bed and went outside in my gown and stomped the prize daylilies Michael had given me on my fortieth birthday. Stomped every bloom till they were all lying in the dirt bruised and broken. The way I feel.

"There now!" I yelled, and then I wiped my feet on the doormat and went upstairs and climbed back into bed. Shaking all over.

It was two o'clock in the morning. I felt like a crazy woman.

I still do, a little bit. I'm just glad the children aren't here to see me.

Daniel would understand, of course. Hannah would be taking steps to help me, calling psychiatrists, that kind of thing, and Emily would be plying me with popcorn and holding cool washcloths to my forehead and telling me everything was going to be all right.

Well...this is not something I will tell Michael, though I try to recount every small detail of my day to him in the hope that he hears and will respond. Who knows how much he hears?

This morning I stopped by the bakery on the corner by the hospital and bought his favorite cinnamon buns. Then when I got to his room, I held them under his nose and said, "Hi, darling, I brought you some breakfast. It's time now to get up and eat."

His eyelashes fluttered. I could swear it. Almost.

Oh, I don't know what to believe anymore. Maybe I'm seeing signs where there are none. Maybe my own desire for his recovery is so great I've become a master of invention.

Yesterday I said to the nurse's aid, "I do believe Michael's feet moved when I was massaging them. Don't you think that's a very good sign?" And she said... Oh, I don't even like to think about what she said. It was too cruel. But then the truth often is.

She said, "Honey, this man has been in a coma for so long if he ever moves, it will be a pure dee miracle."

I won't tell Daniel what she said. He's got his whole congregation praying for a miracle. A prayer vigil, he calls it.

I just wish I had the kind of faith he has. Where did he get it? Maybe from something Mother said or did. Heaven knows, I've been so wrapped up in Michael all my life I pretty much let the children raise themselves. I listened to them and gave them some guidance—I don't mean that I didn't nurture them. But I gave them a freedom that few children have, and I guess that's why they all turned out the way they did. That, plus the fact that Michael and I both adored them, not only for themselves but for the fact that they were a product of our great love.

Our love of the century. Our romance that was never going to end. NEVER.

I'm doing my part to keep it going. I really am. Here is how I've tried to bring Michael back: Tuesday I read Steinbeck to him all day long—Of Mice and Men—his favorite. He always cries at the end, and I was hoping to move him to tears. But of course, I was the only one crying when Lennie looked out over the river for his rabbits and George shot him in the head.

And then on Wednesday, I made orange spice cookies because he could never resist the smell and would always eat five right off the bat, then sneak back to the cookie jar till they were all gone, though he knew darned good and well that I'd made them all especially for him. Anyway, I ended up sitting by his bed eating the whole batch myself and then sitting up the rest of the night trying to relieve myself with Tums.

Well...I blush to think about Thursday. Thursday night, actually. I'd told the hospital staff I was going to spend the night with Michael again, and I'd call them if we needed anything. They're used to that now. Even sanction it. At this point I think they'd welcome anything that would bring him out of his coma, no matter how unorthodox.

Anyhow, I rented a movie called "Giselle's Candy Stick" which just about says it all. Then I put on this little red see-through outfit that Michael bought for me two years ago on Valentine's Day. As a joke, he said, though by the time we finished romping like sixteen-year-olds, neither of us thought of it as a joke.

As I said, I decked myself out like a call girl, then propped a chair against the door just in case and crawled in bed with my husband. Michael, I told him, I brought a little something to jog your memory.

I turned the volume down low so no sound would drift out into the hallway. If anybody heard what was going on in here, they'd think it was a miracle for sure.

I rolled Michael onto his side, being very careful of his tube, and held him close so he could feel my heart beating against his. I wore his favorite perfume so he could smell my skin and my hair. He always loved that.

"Listen, darling," I told him. "This is what I want."

And then I whispered the most outrageous things in his ear. Shocking things, really. Things I'd never even said to him when he was really with me.

I don't know what got into me. Desperation, I guess.

Needless to say, none of it did any good. Michael never moved a muscle, even when I...well, I'm not even going to write that part down. As a matter of fact, I'm trying to forget it.

When I returned the movie, the woman behind the cash register (Mabel is her name, she's been there for years) said, "I hope it worked, Hon," and I said, "Oh, yes." Then I went home and took the scissors to the red outfit and buried the remains in the backyard.

I'm obviously losing my mind.

Chapter Thirty-One

The morning after Jake arrived, Emily decided the most wonderful thing about being in love was how it cast a rosy glow over every single aspect of your life. She woke up feeling so good about herself and the world in general that she was absolutely certain she'd hear good news when she called her mother.

She left Jake in the kitchen in his bare feet, wearing nothing but his underwear and a big apron she'd insisted on lest he scorch all that glorious hair on his chest. Then she went into the den and picked up the phone.

"Hi, Mom. How's everything?" Meaning mostly, How is Dad, but also, How are you?

"I think we're making some progress here, darling. I really do."

Her mother always tried to sound optimistic, which was fine by Emily. She'd always been a big proponent of positive thinking. Unlike Hannah, who was a realist to the bone and Daniel who was something of a dreamer.

"How's that, Mom?

"Well, I've asked the doctors to step up the physical therapy, you know, to prevent atrophy. There's definitely some improved muscle tone and flexibility."

"That's great, Mom."

"Michael's always been such a fit man. He's going to hate it when he wakes up and finds that his body is not in tiptop shape."

"Yes. He will."

They both acted as if Michael Westmoreland would wake up within the next few minutes. And maybe that was the best way to think. Maybe that was better than all the gloom and doom Emily had seen people so often display in situations like this.

"Tell me about you, Emily. What's going on up there in the woods...besides animal rescue?"

Emily laughed, and it felt so good. "I've got bigger things to rescue. Jake's here."

"Wonderful! Oh, Emily, you don't know how relieved that makes me feel. I was afraid you'd let everything that was happening here ruin things for you."

"No, I won't do that."

"Promise?"

"Yes. I promise."

"Good. Life goes on, Em. We can't afford to stop living just because Michael's in a coma."

"What about you, Mom? I don't want to see you cooped up there all the time. It's not good for you."

"I'm not. I go home nearly every night. Sometimes during the day. Just to take a little walk in the woods or sit in the sunshine with a cup of tea."

"What about friends? I'll bet you haven't gone to a single movie or out to a single lunch since Dad's accident."

"Well, no. But I talk to Jane nearly every day, and she comes by the hospital. Clarice stops by every now and then. And Linda."

"That's good. Still—"

"Listen, Emily, I'm okay. I'm just living my life a bit differently now, that's all. But I don't want *you* to, nor Hannah and Daniel. I want things to be as normal as possible for all of you, and I want you to feel free to follow your heart. No matter what. You hear me, Em?"

"I hear you, Mom. And I am. Truly, I am."

"All right, then. Get off the phone and go back to Jake. That's what counts."

"Mom? Tell Dad I love him. Okay?"

"I will, sweetheart. I always do."

When Emily hung up, Jake was standing in the doorway watching her with this *look* on his face. She closed her eyes, praying, she supposed, for guidance. Praying too for selfish reasons. *Don't let anything else come between us,* was what she was praying.

Her brother would be appalled.

"Any new developments, Em?"

"His muscle tone's improving, Mom said, due to therapy."

"That's good."

"Jake—" Emily went to him and put her hands on his face "—this is not going to come between us again. I won't let it. Promise you won't, either."

He studied her for the longest while before answering, and that scared her. But only a little. After the love they'd shared last night and this morning, there was no way she would ever believe that Jake was not going to be in her life forever.

"It won't," he finally said. "I've come to terms with what happened to Michael."

"Good. Then it need not ever be anything between us except a normal conversation. You'll want to know about Dad and I'll want to tell you. From now on it will be that simple."

"How did I ever find such a wise woman?"

"You just got lucky, I guess."

Jake swatted her playfully with a dish towel. When she screeched in mock horror, he picked her up and kissed her until she was breathless, then carried her into the kitchen where they sat on chairs pulled close and he fed her bites of pancake dripping with melted butter and real maple syrup. She felt pampered. And secure. And very well loved.

She thought, This is the most wonderful thing that has ever happened to me. And she vowed she was going to be in love with Jake Bean forever. No matter what.

Jake had always enjoyed puttering around a house, fixing things, and he especially enjoyed it at Emily's. There were so many things that needed fixing, and making repairs for her gave him the sense of being indispensable, heroic even. Mainly, he guessed, because she was so appreciative of every little thing. For instance, the lightbulb he'd changed in her closet because she couldn't reach the fixture even standing on a three-step ladder.

"That's wonderful," she'd said, clapping her hands. Then she'd kissed him to show him exactly how wonderful she thought it was, and they'd ended up making love on the floor, scrunched between her rain boots and her luggage.

The day before, he'd done a simple repair job on her bedside lamp, which she admitted hadn't worked for three months. She'd been too busy to take it to a repair shop, and besides, it was so far away and she used the lamp so seldom, why bother?

Then when it was working, she'd cheered like a little kid. Her often childlike approach to life was a quality Jake found endearing, and the more he saw of her the harder it was for him not to say all the things that were on his heart.

Not yet, all his instincts told him, and he listened. That was the way he was. Though why they had deserted him the day of Michael's accident still remained a mystery to him.

A mystery now, not a thorn that prodded his flesh.

Jake was in the kitchen sharpening all her knives when Emily came into the room fresh from her bath, one towel wrapped around her wet hair and another wrapped around her waist, sarong-style.

"Are you trying to seduce me?" he said.

She posed in the doorway, smiling.

"Yes."

"Well, it's working."

"Good."

She was still in the doorway, her eyes turning that dark and sparkly green they always did when she was aroused. Jake put the knives back in the kitchen drawer one by one, never taking his eyes off Emily. And then he went to her and unwrapped her hair.

It fell to her shoulders in wet dark waves. He lifted it off her neck and kissed away the drops of water that still clung to her warm, scented skin.

"You taste good."

"There's more."

He leaned against the doorjamb, feigning nonchalance.

"Want to give me a hint?"

Her eyes on his, she unknotted the towel at her waist and it fell to the floor.

"So I see."

Jake studied her for a small eternity, memorizing every line. And in fact, that was what he was doing, for tomorrow he would leave to lead an expedition to Dapsang.

"What?" Emily whispered.

"This...and this...and this."

He was touching her everywhere, and then kneeling before her, and the taste of her was like no other, a heady blend of floral scents and the exotic musk of warm slick skin that Jake could sometimes taste even in his dreams, even when he was in Georgia and she was in Mississippi.

Standing, he took her hand and led her into the bedroom, and when she lay down, smiling, and he was over her, inside her looking down, he thought he'd never seen a more beautiful woman. It was not merely physical beauty but an indescribable *something* that shone from her eyes. And for a moment he lost his breath.

He had a sudden vision of himself on a mountain and Emily far away, beyond his reach. Forever.

An unutterable sadness overtook him, and when she reached up and touched his face and asked him what was wrong, he said, "Nothing." Hoping it was true. Praying it was true.

"Well...then...good."

She pulled him down to her and kissed his eyelids and his cheeks and then ever so softly claimed his lips. Jake forgot everything except the moment.

And ecstasy.

As Emily watched Jake pack for his return to Georgia she couldn't help but think of the many times she'd witnessed her mother seeing her father off on yet another journey to a faraway place.

This is all right, she kept telling herself. Everything is

fine between us now, and he will come home safe and sound, and maybe, just maybe he'll say, *I love you, Em.* And then we'll be together forever.

"Emily. I don't want you to walk me to the car. Okay?"

"Well...okay."

"I'm superstitious, I guess."

"I understand, really I do. Dad had his rituals, too."

"Did he?"

"Yes. One of them was to always leave a gift for Mom. Something that would surprise her after he'd gone."

"Such as?"

"Sometimes she'd find a box of candy under the bed-covers, or flowers would be delivered not fifteen minutes after he walked out the door. Once he had a parrot delivered that kept saying, 'I love you, Anne.' It nearly drove us all crazy."

"Whatever happened to it?"

"We never knew. Mom was in the habit of opening his door every morning because she couldn't stand to see a thing caged. Usually the bird would fly around the porch, swoop down into the gardenia bushes, then fly right back into his cage. But one morning he didn't. He flew past the magnolia tree and just kept on going. Seeking freedom, I guess."

"Or adventure." Jake smiled at her. "Like our Gwendolyn."

"I miss her."

"She'll probably come back, if nothing else, to show off her children."

Emily was laughing, then all of a sudden she was crying, in spite of her fierce determination not to. She tried to pretend she was merely sniffing, but Jake caught on to her.

"Hey, no tears. I'll be back before you know it."

"It's not that. Honestly, it's not."

He cupped her face in the tenderest way imaginable and bent close. "What's wrong, Em?"

"I don't know."

And she didn't. Not really. She just had this *feeling*. The kind you get when you're headed to the airport, but you *know* you've already missed your plane.

Jake kissed her, started to go, then leaned down and kissed her again.

"Em, promise me you'll take care of yourself while I'm gone."

"Of course. I always do."

"I'm serious."

"Well, so am I. What do you think I'm going to do? Throw myself in front of a truck or something?"

She made herself laugh to show that she was just kidding and that she had nothing to cry about and that all this was a silly misunderstanding, which wasn't how she wanted to say goodbye to Jake. Not at all.

"I'm sorry, Jake. That came out wrong.... Excuse me."

She ended up having to go into the bathroom and blow her nose on toilet paper, of all things. The indignity of it. And when she went back into the bedroom, Jake was smiling.

"I'm going to get six boxes of tissue and put them in strategic places so my girl will always have one handy."

"You don't mind that I'm the original weeping willow?"

"If anybody ever said such a thing about you, you'd box his ears. At the very least." He pulled her close. "You're not a weeping willow, Emily Westmoreland. You're just like your father. Tough as nails."

"Okay, then. Good. I like that."

"So do I. Very much." He kissed her on the cheek, then on the lips. For a long, long time. "Bye, Em."

"Till we meet again, Jake."

She watched until he was out the door and for a long time afterward. For some reason she wanted to close her eyes and not open them until he got back. Like a little child. Shutting out the world. Keeping everything safe.

"Be safe," she whispered.

Then she picked up the phone to call her mom.

Chapter Thirty-Two

August 30, 2001

I've started sleeping in Michael's shirts. Every one of them. One after the other.

Here's what I do: I leave him at the hospital still sleeping as peacefully as a child, then go home, open his closet and press my face into his shirts, all hanging useless now. I take deep breaths, hoping to catch the familiar scent of him, but it has been so long since he's worn them that all I can smell is starch.

Then I strip and wrap one of his shirts around me like arms. Holding me close. I climb into bed and curl up in a ball, tucking as much of my body as possible inside Michael's shirt. Then I cry. For fear that he will never wear them again.

It has been so long! Summer is almost gone. He missed the gardenias and the roses, the lilies and the asters, the

night-blooming moon vine and the sweetly scented di-
anthus.

I picked them all and carried them to the hospital,
hoping the scents would arouse him. But of course, it
didn't work, and now the dreadful heat of August combined with an awful season of drought has taken its toll,
and the garden is stripped of bloom. Browning and bar-
ren.

It looks the way I feel.

Daniel was alarmed when he came last weekend and
saw me. He said, "We must not lose faith."

And oh, I know he's right. I know. Still I have to
search very hard inside myself to find a little leftover
hope.

Even the doctors are losing hope. I can tell.

And yet...and yet, Michael still looks healthy. With
regular therapy, he is fairly fit and toned. Thanks to his
naturally olive skin and many hours burning in the sun
and snow, he doesn't have the pallor of a sick man but
the swarthy look of a man who might have just come in
from the garden and stretched out to take a nap.

Hannah is still in Yellowstone on assignment, but Emily is here for a few days. Glowing, I might add. Thank
goodness.

Jake's in the Himalayas once more, and she carries a
letter from him around in her purse. I asked her to read
it to Michael, the parts that deal with his latest climb. I
told her he doesn't hear enough about the mountains. I
said, "Maybe that's what he needs to get through the
darkness that still holds him prisoner."

Emily sat by Michael's bed and held his hand, and
before she started to read, this is what she said to him:

"Now, Dad, I want you to pay close attention because
you're the expert, and if Jake's not doing something

right, I want to know about it. I want you tell me so we can correct the situation. I'm in love with him, you know, and I want him to always come back to me. The way you always come back to Mom.''

Well, I had a hard time holding back tears when she said that. Thank goodness I was standing behind her and she didn't see me wiping my face. She'd have understood, though. Emily's like me in that respect. Emotional.

Michael used to call tears my safety valve. He'd say, ''Releasing those tears keeps you from exploding, my love.''

He was right, of course. During the whole course of our marriage I never once raised my voice to him. Not once. Nor he to me. I always told him if anything bothered me, and he always listened. And when I cried, he held me close and dried my tears with the tips of his fingers and told me, ''You go ahead and cry, angel. I'm here, holding on to you.''

My Michael is so wise, so compassionate.

Well, anyway, back to Jake's letter.

He told about the people in his latest expedition, about how he'd always screened them carefully. About how he was growing suspicious that one of the women in his group had lied about her climbing credentials, particularly since she didn't seem to know an ice ax from a butter knife.

Jake made light of the whole thing in his letter, of course, and had both of us laughing, but lack of experience is a serious matter on an unforgiving mountain. I didn't say that to Emily, though. I didn't want to worry her.

And she's so giddy right now with her love I don't think she thought of it. Or maybe she just doesn't know.

You see, when Michael climbed, I didn't talk about the dangers to my children. I wanted them to think of their father as merely being off on the job, the way a CPA goes to his office or a farmer goes to his fields.

The main thing is that Emily is happy. All my children have settled back into their lives. That doesn't mean they're not worried about Michael, of course, or that they love him any less.

Life goes on, that's all. I've told them that many times, and if he could talk that's what he'd tell them, too.

Nobody knows how long this thing will go on, nor when it will be over.

The thing is, I'm prepared for the long haul. Or at least I think I am.

There are all these tricks I have to keep myself going. One of them is to listen to Michael's voice on the answering machine. "Hello, you've reached Michael and Anne Westmoreland. Leave a message and we'll get back to you."

I play that over and over. I hear his dear voice and think of the thousand messages I've left him since he's been in the hospital. The thousand things I've said to try to bring him back.

"I love you, Michael," that's what I always say. Then I say, "Do you hear me? If you do, why don't you get back to me? Why don't you answer me? Wake up, Michael. Please, please wake up."

Chapter Thirty-Three

Jake and his party had only been on the mountain four days before the inexperience of one of the climbers became obvious. Rosalee Edmunds, who had presented herself as a "veteran of the world's most challenging peaks, including Everest," had neither the stamina nor the strength and expertise to reach the summit of Dapsang.

Rather than make a scene, Jake decided to have a private talk with her at the end of the day's climb. While the rest of his crew and clients were resting, he asked Rosalee to join him in his tent.

She was so exhausted when she sat down he thought she was going to fall right to sleep. There were two ways Jake could approach her: soft pedal or get straight to the point.

He chose the latter.

"Mrs. Edmunds," he said, "it's clear to me that you're not going to be able to make it to the summit."

"Oh, but I will. I promise you."

"I'm not looking for promises here. I'm dealing with reality. The fact is, you're slowing down this climb, and that puts the rest of my party in danger. I'm going to send you back down the mountain with Jamal Tongay."

"I'm not going."

"He's my right-hand man, Mrs. Edmunds, one of the best natural climbers I've ever seen. You'll be perfectly safe with him. You'll be safe at base camp until we pick you up on our return trip."

"You don't understand, Mr. Bean. It's not my safety I'm concerned about. Nor yours, either, for that matter. I paid money for you to get me to the top of this damned mountain, and that's where I'm going."

"There's a storm brewing, Mrs. Edmunds. Already our window of opportunity is narrowing. With you in the climb, the party has no hope of gaining the summit."

"That's not my problem, Mr. Bean. That's yours."

"Exactly. That's why I'm sending you back."

"Oh, but you're not. That is, unless you want to have a lawsuit on your hands that will tie you up in court for so long you might never see the summit of another mountain."

Her threat was not an idle one. She was married to one of the most powerful lawyers in Georgia. Obviously she was on the climb for one reason and one only. Bragging rights.

He'd heard other guides talking about it, the society matrons they'd dragged to the tops of mountains. Men, too. People who had no business on a mountain in the first place.

He'd prided himself on never taking one of them in his party, and now he had only himself to blame. He usually screened more carefully. Lately, though, he'd been so preoccupied he hadn't done his usual thorough job. He should have double-checked Rosalee Edmunds.

"Threats don't work with me, Mrs. Edmunds."

"Mr. Bean, the only way I'm going back down this mountain is kicking and screaming all the way. Now, unless you want that kind of scene on your hands, unless you want to add assault to the list of charges I'll bring against you, I suggest we all get some sleep so we'll be ready to start fresh in the morning."

Rosalee Edmunds got up and walked out.

That was why, the next morning, she was still in the climbing party. With Jamal Tongay as her personal guide.

"I'll carry her up the mountain on my back if necessary," he'd told Jake. "If we drop behind, you and the rest of the party push on. That way you have a chance of reaching the summit and Mrs. Edmunds is placated."

Jake had agreed, but against his better judgment. Then he'd put his second-best Sherpa climber in Jamal's place and resumed his push to the top.

The sixth day out, Jamal and Rosalee had dropped so far behind they were out of sight. The winds had picked up speed. Jake studied the situation, briefly considered turning and heading back down the mountain, then decided to continue.

They were making good time now that Rosalee was not in the party. They might just make it.

When Emily saw her mother coming up the sidewalk, she raced into the living room to make sure everything was in order, then turned on the stereo, adjusted her skirt and flung open the door.

"Good grief!" Anne stepped back and stood under the porch light. "What's going on?"

"We're going to Hawaii, that's what."

"Well, of course, Michael and I will go when he..."
She covered her mouth with her hand as if she could hold
back the pain, and Emily grabbed her arm and pulled her
into the house.

"Here, put this on."

Emily thrust a grass skirt and coconut bra at her mother.
Exactly like the one she was wearing. Hannah had brought
them back from Hawaii four years ago when she was there
on assignment. She'd also brought some CDs of Polynesian
music, and that was what was playing now, "Maori Blue
Eyes," which the three of them had played one evening
after supper while they attempted the hula. Their audience
of two, Michael and Daniel, had doubled over laughing.

Anne held the skirt at arm's length. "I'd forgotten about
these."

"Put it on."

At first Emily thought her mother was going to protest,
then she said, "Why not?"

"Great. Things need lightening up around here."

"Right." Anne held the coconut bra in front of her
blouse. "I've gained weight since I wore this last. I'll probably spill out of it."

"Sexy. I'll take a snapshot so Dad can see it."

She actually did take a picture when her mother came
back looking better than any woman of fifty-something had
a right to look.

"I only hope I hold up as well as you," Emily said.

"Hush. You make me sound like an old fossil."

"Do you remember the steps, Mom?" Emily began to
sway her hips to the music.

"We made them up, with Hannah choreographing, so
you know what that means."

What it meant was they might or might not have been
doing the real hula. Give Hannah one shot at something,

and she fancied herself an expert. That was how she was. Self-confident is what she called herself, but Emily sometimes called her bullheaded.

"Who cares whether they're right or not?" Emily picked up the plastic ukulele she'd found in the back of the closet in Hannah's room. Another of her sister's attempts at knowing everything. She plucked a sour note or two, then began swaying around the room.

"Come on, Mom. Get with the program."

"We look ridiculous, you know.

"Yeah, I know. That's what makes it so much fun."

Her mother stood by the piano watching, while Emily made a fool of herself. She was beginning to think her plan to bring some fun back into her mother's life was a total failure when all of a sudden Anne let out a whoop and started twirling around the room, hips rotating like Elvis and grass skirt going ninety to nothing.

They danced until they were both too tired to move, then they collapsed onto the floor, holding on to each other and laughing.

Emily wished Jake and her dad were there with them, but she caught herself right before she said so. There would be no sadness tonight. That was what she'd decided after she'd left her mother at the hospital. Nothing said to remind both of them of what they'd lost.

"Lord, these coconut shells are pinching me," Anne said. "If I don't get out of them, I'm going to be two bra sizes smaller."

"Wait. Don't take off your costume."

"Why not?"

"Because we're going to a luau."

"Where?"

"In the kitchen."

"Don't tell me you've pit-roasted a whole pig in the kitchen?"

"No, but I did bake ham with pineapple."

"For this I have to wear a coconut bra?"

"Why not?"

"Indeed, why not?"

Anne linked arms with her daughter, and they hulaed all the way to the kitchen, hips keeping time to the music.

All in all, Emily considered the evening a roaring success. She couldn't wait until Jake came home so she could tell him about it.

The storm struck as Jake and his party were going back down the mountain.

Fortunately he'd climbed using the siege strategy, and they were not far from Camp II in the lee of a huge dome-shaped rock that would not be whited out unless the storm escalated. And if that happened, they were all doomed.

All, that is, except Jamal and Rosalee. They had never caught up with Jake's team. Knowing Jamal, he would have long since departed for the camp.

That was Jake's hope as he led his party through the storm. His hope and his prayer.

"Everybody, stick close," he yelled, though he wasn't certain how much his clients heard over the howling wind.

Still, he wasn't overly concerned about them. Long before the full force of the storm stuck, he'd paired his clients with his Sherpa team, who knew the mountain like the back of their hand.

Besides, Jake could already make out a huge shadow emerging through the storm. Dome rock. An enormous flagship wallowing through the waves of snow.

He gained the last few hundred feet, then flung open the tent flap, calling, "Jamal!"

The tent was empty. Jake went back outside, cupped his hands and screamed, "Jamal!" No beaming brown face emerged from any of the tents. No gold-toothed smile greeted him.

Frantic, Jake did a tent-by-tent search. Jamal and Rosalee were nowhere to be found.

As the rest of his party straggled in two-by-two, Jake called his four best Sherpas into his tent for a conference.

"Has anybody had radio contact with Jamal?"

They all shook their heads, and Jake's spirits fell.

Somewhere out in the storm were his best Sherpa guide and one of his clients. In all his years of guiding, he'd never lost anybody.

It happened. He heard about it all the time from other guides, many of whom had more experience than he did. Excellent climbers. Responsible men.

Jake had always marveled at how they accepted such loss as part of the price they paid for challenging the world's toughest mountains. He used to wonder what he would do if it ever happened to him.

"You're just lucky, Jake." That was what fellow climber and mountain guide Rufus Plummer had told him.

And now, it seemed, his luck had run out.

"No!" he shouted.

The only reaction he got from his unflappable Sherpas was some rapid blinking and respectful stares.

"We'll organize a search party," he told them. "Jamal and Rosalee are somewhere on this mountain, and we're going to find them."

Or die trying.

He didn't say that. It was something all of them knew.

Chapter Thirty-Four

Emily and her mother had finally ditched their hula costumes in favor of pajamas. They were sprawled on the sofa with two big bowls of gingered pineapple sorbet Emily had picked up on the way home from the hospital.

She was pleasantly tired, replete with delicious food, limp with laughter and all in all feeling good. Jake would be coming home soon, and then, except for her father, Emily's life would be perfect.

She flipped through the TV guide searching for a good late-night movie.

"How about this?" she asked her mother. "*Cyrano*, with Jose Ferrer and Mala Powers? It won an Academy Award."

"Sounds good to me."

Emily padded to the TV barefoot and switched it on. The late-night-news broadcast was playing. She popped the movie into the VCR and was getting ready to change channels when Tom Brokaw caught her attention.

"Rosalee Edmunds, wife of renowned criminal attorney Ralph Edmunds of Atlanta disappeared in the Himalayan mountains yesterday, along with her Sherpa guide Jamal Tongay."

"That's Jake's guide."

Emily turned up the volume, then sat on the floor with her arms wrapped around herself.

"Mrs. Edmunds was a member of the party Jake Bean led into K2, the world's second-highest mountain. Bean and a team of Sherpas have gone back into the storm that overtook the giant mountain in an attempt to locate the missing pair."

Going into a storm in the mountains carried with it the grave risk of never coming back. Some of the world's most renowned climbers had died that way.

Emily started shaking all over and crying without sound. Tears streamed down her cheeks and pooled in the corners of her mouth. She tasted salt and bitter regret.

She thought of all the beautiful things she'd wanted to say to Jake and hadn't. She thought of the many ways she could have shown him she loved him, but didn't.

Why hadn't she told him more often "I love you"? Why hadn't she told him she wanted to be with him forever, no matter what? Why hadn't she told him she thought he was the most wonderful man in the world and that she'd simply die without him?

"Emily…" Her mother sat on the floor beside her, then draped an afghan over both of them. "I know, I know."

In the warm cocoon of wool they leaned their heads together and cried.

At her mother's insistence, Emily spent the night in Anne's big bed. Mostly awake. What little sleep she got was fitful, so that when she got up early the next morning, she was so bleary-eyed she could barely see the controls on the TV.

Rescue attempts in the Himalayans were on all the channels.

"Today the search continues for two people lost on K2, the world's second-highest mountain." That from Channel Three. Channel Five was running photographs of the missing twosome, as well as a recent shot of Jake. "World-renowned climber and mountain guide" is what they called him.

Channel Six out of Jackson, Mississippi, ran the same shots of Jake, plus some of "the best high-altitude film-maker of our century, Michael Westmoreland, who lies in a coma. He was doing an IMAX film starring Jake Bean when..."

A sound in the doorway made Emily turn. Her mother was standing there like a marble statue, staring at the television screen. Emily switched it off.

"I'm sorry, Mom."

"There's nothing for you to be sorry about. Michael is still news. He'll be happy to hear that."

"Mom—"

"Turn the TV back on. We need to know what's happening with Jake."

Emily switched back to Channel Six. "No word has yet been heard from Jake Bean, who is leading the search party for Edmunds and the Sherpa guide."

"That's not necessarily bad," Anne said. "He's too busy fighting the mountain to worry about radio contact. Do you want pancakes for breakfast?"

"I'm not hungry."

"You need to eat, anyhow." Her mother pulled out the skillet, then began stirring batter. Over her shoulder, she said, "You'll probably hear good news by noon today. I'll stay here with you."

"No, I don't want you to do that. You need to be with Dad."

"You're sure? I can call Jane or Clarice to go over there for a little while."

"What if this is the day Dad wakes up? You'd never forgive yourself for not being there. And I'd never forgive myself, either. No, Mom, you go ahead. I'll be fine."

"You're sure?"

"Absolutely."

She smiled for her mother's benefit, but inside she felt like shattered glass.

She also ate a few bites of pancake so her mother wouldn't worry, then she glued herself to the TV to listen for news, any news at all, while her mother dressed, then left for the hospital.

Emily must have dozed, for she jerked awake in time to hear the news reporter say, "There is no word yet from the Himalayan rescue party led by Jake Bean. Hope dims for the stranded climbers, as well as the members of the search party."

"Noooo!" Emily screamed, and the grandfather clock in the hall struck twelve, underscoring her distress.

As she sat in the kitchen with her scream echoing through the house, she came to the startling realization that she was constitutionally unsuited to being a climber's wife. Even a climber's lover.

How had her mother managed all those years? That was what Emily wanted to know, and that was what she'd ask as soon as Anne came home.

Meanwhile she had the rest of the day to get through. The only way she figured she could do that was under anesthesia. The liquid kind.

She selected a good chardonnay and was in the process of finding the corkscrew when all of a sudden she saw herself for what she was. A hypocrite.

Here she was planning on getting skunk drunk because she was too chicken to face the possibility of losing Jake, when she'd been the one to encourage her mother to dance and laugh and go on with life while she faced the same frightening prospect. Losing Michael.

She banged the cabinet door open and stowed the unopened bottle of wine.

She remembered the first time her father ever got in trouble on a mountain. Emily had been six years old, and she'd never seen her mother cry so much. Constantly, it seemed. Hours on end.

Until Grandmother Beaufort came over. She'd taken one look at Anne, put her hands on her hips and yelled, "Plant flowers! Bake a cake! Paint the library! Dammit, Anne, do anything except sit around feeling sorry for yourself. I brought you up better than that. The Beauforts face adversity with courage and grace."

Emily had never heard her grandmother use a byword. In fact, she and Hannah had been roundly lectured by her for calling Glennella Moody a "derned snob." "If you can't say something nice about somebody, don't say anything at all," she'd told them.

So the day her grandmother had said dammit stuck in Emily's mind as Important Lessons Number One, Two and Three. Stay busy, abstain from self-pity and keep your chin up.

Emily washed her face, put on some shorts, then drove to the nursery and bought a carload of flowers. Never mind that it was August and hot as the hinges of hell. Never mind that the plants would all commit suicide within the next week or so.

Tomorrow could take care of itself. Today she was going to plant flowers.

She was still in the garden when Anne drove up around sunset. Her mother stood for a while without saying anything, then finally she said, "I've always liked pansies."

"It's a good thing, since you now have about two hundred."

Anne squatted beside her and draped an arm over her shoulders.

"I see you took Mother's advice."

"Yes."

"Sometimes I think she's the wisest woman I know." Anne took a clean handkerchief from her pocket and wiped the sweat and grime off Emily's face. "What do you say we go in the house and make a tall pitcher of lemonade? Then I'll tell you about my day."

"And I'll tell you about mine."

Anne laughed. "I already know what you did with your day."

"Except for the hard part. Mom, I've done a lot of thinking. About my relationship with Jake. About what will happen if...*when* he comes home."

"I know. I know."

"You do?"

"Of course. Don't you think I had the same reservations about marrying your father?"

"You did?"

"Absolutely. I'll let you read some more of my old diary, if that will help, but first I want you to think about whether your love is strong enough to withstand this kind of challenge. You know he'll keep going back to the mountain, and if you can't handle it, you should back out now. Before the marriage."

"Jake hasn't asked me to marry him."

"He will."

"He hasn't even told me he loves me."

"Honey, don't you know that the good men take a long time saying that? They don't want to put anything in words until they are absolutely certain they won't want to take it back."

They skirted around the pansies Emily had put in containers because she'd run out of room in the flower beds—pots and pots of them in every shade of purple, which was one of Emily's favorite colors. And fortunately Anne's, too.

"How's Dad?" she asked as soon as they were in the kitchen and she'd come back from washing her hands and face.

"He's still not awake, but I know Michael is in there somewhere. I can *feel* him. And as long as I can feel his spirit, I have hope."

Emily thought about Jake, vanished somewhere on that vast mountain.

"There's always hope," she said.

And there was. Oh, there was.

Chapter Thirty-Five

December 19, 1966

I'm supposed to marry Michael tomorrow, and all of a sudden I have cold feet. Mother says every bride-to-be gets them, but I don't think she understands the extent of my fear. This is not ordinary jitters; this is a bone-chilling fear that I'm going to be marrying a man who is already married—to the mountains. It's a gut-wrenching feeling that the minute I say "I do," a horrible fate will befall him in some faraway land and I'll be a widow before I've had time to put away the wedding gown.

Here's what happened: I was at the beauty salon getting my hair cut before the wedding, and Merlene had the television going ninety-to-nothing, which is what she always does because so many of her customers like to watch the game shows. I was sitting in the chair waiting my turn, thumbing through an out-of-date magazine with my mind only halfway occupied, when all of a sudden a news bulletin interrupted the game show.

"Fifteen people are dead on Mount McKinley in the worst climbing accident of this century."

That's what the television reporter said, and I made a complete fool of myself. Dropped the magazine in the middle of the floor and stood up with my hand over my mouth, holding back a scream.

Michael was nowhere near a mountain. I knew that. And yet suddenly I had a vision of him lying dead in the snow on Mount McKinley. Frozen stiff. Every part of him, even his beautiful smile.

Merlene came up to me and said, "Are you all right, hon?" and I nodded and told her I was fine. But the truth was, I was trembling so hard inside I thought I would break into pieces.

I picked up the magazine and put it back in the rack, then headed for the door. Merlene caught up with me and said, "Where are you going, hon? I thought you wanted your hair cut." And I said that I changed my mind.

I had to see Michael. I had to touch him. I had to know that he was alive, that he was not buried under ice and snow. I had to hear him tell me that he would *never* die on top of a mountain.

Somewhere between the beauty salon and the hotel where Michael was staying before the wedding, I regained my sanity.

Of course, I couldn't go to him in the state I was in. I had too much pride to present myself as some kind of hysterical woman. And so I went home, instead.

That's when Mother told me about bride-to-be jitters.

That was before I told her everything, though, before I told her about the tragedy on McKinley.

She just looked at me after I told her all that, and then she said, "Anne, nobody is ever guaranteed tomorrow. You can live your life in one of two ways: You can play it safe in the vain hope that you've avoided all possibility of tragedy and pain, or you can take the risks and let the angels take care of the rest. Now you tell me which one you're going to do, because if you're not going to marry Michael Westmoreland, I'm going to take that high-priced dress I bought for the reception back and get a refund."

"Well, of course, I'm going to marry Michael. Tomorrow."

That's what I told her, and all of a sudden I knew it was true, and that it was right.

I love him so much that I'd rather have only a few months with him, a few days, a few hours, than a lifetime with anyone else.

To play it safe would consign me to a half-life, a sort of tranquilized existence where the door is shut to great joy, as well as great pain.

To take the risks will be to embrace joy and pain equally, but through it all to know that I am living my life fully and passionately, to know that my soul and spirit are alive and well and that my heart is rising on wings of eagles.

And so tomorrow I will stand before the JP with my beloved where we will exchange the vows we've written. None of this "in sickness and health" bit, "till death do us part," which is so dour and Puritan-sounding. No, we will pledge to enter into a union that honors the spirit and respects the soul. Our love is true and strong and enduring, and we will pledge to nurture it and to keep the flame always burning.

Chapter Thirty-Six

The storm on the mountain was nothing compared to the phalanx of reporters waiting at the base of Dapsang. When Jake saw them he momentarily considered trying to slip through the crowd unnoticed, but that would be the coward's way out.

He was responsible for what had happened on that mountain, and he would face the music.

"There he is!" a veteran reporter on the front lines shouted, then raced to Jake. "Mr. Bean, can you tell us the condition of Rosalee Edmunds and Jamal Tongay?"

It was the one question Jake had been dreading. Word had preceded the search party that the two had been found. Until Jake told exactly what had happened, everything else was speculative.

"Considering how long she was exposed to the storm, Mrs. Edmunds is in good condition—thanks to Jamal Tongay. Right now she's suffering from altitude sickness and dehydration, but she will recover and be perfectly fine.''

"What about Tongay?''

Pain sliced through Jake like a knife blade. When he'd found them, Jamal's body had been literally covering and protecting Rosalee. And when he'd seen the condition of his most trusted climber, he'd cried, and the tears had frozen on his face.

Jake would gladly have given everything he owned if he could turn back the clock and undo his decision. For it had been his decision that put Jamal at the mercy of the mountain. His and his alone.

And for that he would always suffer. Not a day would go by that he wouldn't remember that he was the one responsible for taking away Jamal's first and greatest love, as well as his livelihood.

"Jamal Tongay will lose his right hand and his right leg. He sacrificed them for Rosalee Edmunds.''

"Will he ever climb again?''

"No.''

"Can you tell me exactly what happened on that mountain?''

How can you describe hell? That was Jake's first thought. His second was, You don't. You keep it inside where it belongs.

"No,'' he told the reporter, then turned to leave.

"Mr. Bean…Mr. Bean…''

The reporters raced after him like a pack of wolves. Jake turned around to face them, a tall angry man, his eyes reddened by blinding snow and lack of sleep, his face raw from exposure and his heart hurting.

"I have no further comment.''

* * *

Transfixed, Emily gripped the arms of her chair and leaned toward the television screen as if she might be able to get close enough to touch Jake.

"He made it, he made it."

She kept whispering that over and over.

"Yes, he did. How do you feel about everything now, Emily?"

"What are you asking me, Mom?"

"What happened on that mountain might never happen again. Jake could lead a charmed life and come back from every climb with nothing except great memories and a huge sense of accomplishment. But chances of that are slim."

"I know."

"Well, then...do you love him enough to suffer for him?"

Her mother didn't have to explain. Emily knew what she meant.

Over the past two days Emily had not only suffered for herself, she'd suffered for Jake. She agonized for all she imagined he was going through both physically and emotionally. Although she'd been at Belle Rose in Vicksburg in one of the hottest summers on record, she'd lived in a frozen place, where bitter cold enveloped not only the body but the spirit.

"Yes," she said, and she meant it with all her heart.

"Then you must go to him. You must be there when he comes home...to save him from himself."

"I know, I know."

"Guilt is going to eat him alive. Even worse this time, I think, than when Michael got caught in that avalanche. If you aren't there, he might withdraw from you and never come back."

Emily could see the pain that talking about the accident was causing her mother.

"Mom, you don't have to talk about it."

"Facts are facts, Emily. Avoiding the truth won't change them."

"I know, but still—"

"Jake will need you, Emily, and you will need him."

"What should I do? What can I say?"

"Make your plane reservations, that's what you should do. He'll be home any day now. As for the rest, you'll know what to say when the time comes."

When his plane touched down in Atlanta, Jake thought about going straight to the ticket counter and buying another ticket to Southern California or Mexico or even Hawaii. Somewhere as far away from mountains as he could get. Also someplace where the phone wouldn't ring, reporters wouldn't camp outside his door, and well-meaning neighbors wouldn't ask nosy questions.

The more he thought about that option, the more he liked it. To heck with his checked luggage. He'd get that after he got his ticket.

To Mexico. That was it. He'd cross the border, drink tequila and try to forget.

He was emerging from the jetway when he saw her. Emily. The person he wanted to see most in the world.

And least.

He wasn't ready for her. Not yet. Maybe not ever again.

Flying halfway around the world gave a man plenty of time to think, and the conclusion he'd come to was that he was jinxed. It had all started around the time he'd met Emily, and maybe that was the universe's way of telling him that he was not meant to have somebody in his life. Maybe that was fate saying, You're supposed to be alone, and you knew it all the time.

She'd already seen him, of course. He stood head and

shoulders above the rest of the crowd coming off the plane. There was no way he could duck and run.

Besides, it would be cowardly.

What to do? What to say?

She smiled at him, then gave a little two-fingered wave. Smart girl. She didn't call attention to him by shouting out his name.

Not that any reporters knew he was on the plane. Still...

"I'm glad you're home," Emily said.

She stood quietly in front of him and touched his hand. That was all. A sweet, simple touch that electrified him.

How was he ever going to leave her?

"Thank you." What else was there to say?

He hadn't expected her to be there. When he'd called to tell her he was safe, she hadn't said anything about meeting his plane, nor had he asked. In fact, he'd been very careful not to mention seeing her at all.

As much as he wanted to. As much as he wanted to hold on to her and never let go.

"I drove," she said. "There are groceries in the car. I thought you'd want to be quiet for a few days."

"Yes, I do."

"Jake..." She looked at him for a long time, then shook her head. "We'll talk later. Let's get your bags and go home."

This was the part Jake dreaded. He'd pictured himself going home and crashing. And then later, before he deplaned he'd imagined himself running off to Mexico.

She stood quietly beside him while he got his bags, and for that, he was grateful.

When they were in the car, she said, "You must be exhausted. I'll drive. Just give me directions."

He said, "Good," then told her how to get to his apartment and leaned his head against the seat.

"I don't remember ever being this tired," he said, and the next thing he knew they were at his apartment and she was leaning over him with this wonderful, loving look on her face.

For a moment Jake thought he was in her bed at the cabin in Mississippi, and he cupped her face and kissed her softly on the lips.

"Hello," he said.

"Hello, right back."

Her smile was a beautiful thing, blooming across her face with such hope and love he wanted to cry. Because that was when he remembered Dapsang. That was when he remembered Jamal, who had smiled bravely at him and said, "It's not your fault, Jake. The mountain takes what she wants, and she wanted part of me."

It was too late to take back the kiss, and so Jake made light of it.

"You're nicer than an alarm clock. Where were you when I needed you in Dapsang?"

He should have stopped with the alarm-clock comment, but he hadn't, and he didn't know why. Fatigue, maybe. Or such gut-deep truth that it wouldn't be denied.

He *had* wanted her in Dapsang. That last day on the mountain right before he'd found Rosalee and Jamal, when he'd known he would die if he extended the search beyond the next few hours, he'd found himself whispering her name over and over, whispering her name and needing her with an intensity that was almost painful.

"I was right there beside you, Jake, every step of the way." She placed one hand over her heart and another over his. "In my heart and yours."

She spoke the truth. It was a truth Jake had skirted around for months now, and if he had been in top form both physically and mentally, he'd have skirted it once again. But in his vulnerable condition, it pierced straight through him, and he knew he loved her. Had loved her from the moment he met her, standing on the lawn at Belle Rose with a skunk peering around her long, tanned legs.

With every atom in his body he yearned to tell her. But he couldn't. A vast, unforgiving mountain stood in the way. Two mountains, really. Dapsang and Everest. Twin burdens of guilt.

Emily was watching him with such sweet concern he wanted to weep. And maybe he would. Later. Alone in the dark. Maybe that was what he needed.

"Let's go inside," she said, and Jake got the bags from the car. "I'm going to make chicken soup. Grandmother Beaufort says it's good for the soul."

"Just what I need."

"Plus this." Emily stood on tiptoe and leaned her head against his chest, then hugged him. Simply hugged him. Without expectations.

And Jake understood the miracle of being in love with a giving woman.

"You rest," she said. "I'll cook."

"I'll just take a short nap."

He kissed her on the cheek, then went into his bedroom, closed the door and fell into the blessed oblivion of sleep.

Chapter Thirty-Seven

Jake's soup was stone cold. Plus, Emily had already had three servings. She'd heard that was how people got fat, eating because they were nervous and didn't know what else to do.

Jake had been asleep five hours. What time was it?

Emily looked at the clock for the fortieth time. It was almost eleven. She was getting sleepy, herself. And grumpy.

Should she get a blanket and stretch out on the sofa, or should she go into Jake's bedroom and risk waking him? She puttered around the kitchen, cleaning countertops that were already so clean you could do surgery on them, straightening teacups in the cabinet. That sort of thing.

Well, if this had been BD, before Dapsang, she'd have gone straight to his bedroom without a single qualm. And so that was what she was going to do. Trust her instincts.

And every instinct she had was screaming at her, If you wait for a sign from Jake, you'll be waiting forever.

She eased open the door and stood in the doorway until her eyes adjusted to the dark. Jake was sleeping on his side with one arm flung over his face. Fully clothed.

Emily tiptoed to the bed and lay down beside him. The bedsprings squeaked but he didn't stir. That was a good thing. What would he think?

Well, it was too late to wonder about that now. She was already in his bed, and so she did the next natural thing. She spooned herself against his back and put her arms around him.

This was right. She could tell by the sense of peace that stole over her, the feeling that she'd come home after a long and difficult journey. What did it matter that he hadn't invited her or that he hadn't said a single thing about loving her and wanting her there with him? She *knew*. That was all.

A woman can always tell whether a man loves her. She can feel it in her bones.

Emily sighed, and then she and her contented bones drifted into sleep.

Jake woke up, stretched, then felt the soft weight against his back. Emily. He stopped in midstretch and eased away so he could see her. She was still in her jeans, and her shirt was crumpled unmercifully. In the half-light of dawn he could see a reddish spot on her cheek where it had rubbed against a seam of his shirt.

The tenderness he felt was a dangerous thing. For both of them.

Jake eased out of bed, being careful not to wake her, then went to the bathroom and closed the door. He didn't even turn on the light, but splashed water on his face and his neck, trying to wake up and cool down at the same time.

The thing that most surprised him was not his tenderness, but his passion. It was not only surprising, but damned inconvenient.

How could he be strong in the face of such a wise and loving woman when his own body insisted on betraying him?

He was easing through the bedroom when he noticed that he'd pulled the covers off Emily, so he went back to the bed and was in the process of pulling them back up when she startled awake.

"Jake?" Her arms were around him immediately, her face pressed into his neck. "I thought I'd lost you."

Was she dreaming? Was he?

"Shh, it was only a dream."

"Mmm," she murmured, then her body went slack and he lowered her back to the bed and covered her with the quilt.

He was sweating when he got to the kitchen. Was it because of his narrow escape or because he'd become so acclimated to the cold that his house in Atlanta felt like a hotbox? Probably some of both.

Jake went into the hall and adjusted the thermostat. Then, feeling guilty, he tiptoed into the bedroom and pulled another quilt out of the closet to cover Emily.

Back in the kitchen he put on coffee, got himself a cup, rambled in the refrigerator for cream and found the soup. She'd made soup for him and he hadn't even had the courtesy to eat it.

"I'm sorry," he said, then felt like a fool for apologizing to a plastic-covered dish of cold soup.

He would have breakfast. That always made him feel better. Eating nutritious foods. Starting the day right.

Emily had stocked his cabinets with three varieties of cereal, plus bagels, and his refrigerator with bacon and eggs, plus cream cheese.

Well, he had no reason to complain. And yet the sight of all that food made him feel even guiltier. And surly. It made him want to go down to the deli on the corner and stuff himself with sugar-glazed doughnuts dripping with grease, and then down three cups of black coffee so strong it would put a bitter taste in his mouth for two hours.

She'd probably wake up while he was gone and wonder where he was, and eventually when he got back he'd feel guiltier still.

Jake sighed. Maybe he ought to just go back to sleep. Maybe he could sleep for the next week or two, and when he woke up Michael would be out of his coma and Jamal would miraculously be ensconced in some new job that paid twice what he'd earned on the mountain, and he would call to say, "Losing my right hand and a leg was the best thing that ever happened to me."

Maybe that was what would happen. And maybe pigs could fly.

Jake poured too much cream in his coffee and was trying to decide whether to pour it down the drain and start over when Emily said, "Jake—"

He dropped his cup. Coffee went everywhere and the cup shattered on the kitchen floor.

They both grabbed dishcloths and knelt at the same time. Their shoulders clashed and their arms got tangled.

"I'll get it," she said.

"No! I'll do it." She jumped as if he'd slapped her. "Just sit over there... Please."

She sat down at the table and didn't say anything while he wiped up the coffee. Well...that was a rotten way to start the day.

The mood he was in, Jake figured things would go down-hill from there.

"I'm sorry, Em. I didn't mean to snap at you."

"That's all right."

"No, it's not." He flung the dishcloth into the sink, then leaned back against the cabinet and faced her. "I'm acting like a jerk, and there's no excuse for it."

"After what you've been through, I don't wonder."

"It's no more than what dozens of climbers have already been through, and what dozens more will go through. Danger, tragedy, disaster—it's all part of my job, Emily, and if I can't handle it, then I might as well get off the mountain and stay home."

"Is that what you want?"

"Is it what you want, Em? For me to quit climbing?"

She didn't say anything. Just watched him with wide, wet-looking eyes.

"Is that why you came here? To convince me to give up this foolishness and do something that's safe and sane?"

"I don't deserve that, Jake."

"No, you don't. You deserve someone who will be there at night when you go to bed and still be there when you wake up in the morning."

"Why are you doing this? Why are you saying these things?"

"I'm just telling the truth."

They stared at each other, and the silence was so thick you could almost see it.

"I came here because I love you, Jake. I want you to know that. I love you no matter what you decide to do. I'll always love you."

She waited. Hoping, he supposed, that he would return her declarations. It would be so easy. All he had to do was tell her how he felt.

"Disaster is dogging my footsteps, Em. I won't subject you to that any longer."

She took a deep, trembling breath. He could see the effort it took to keep her composure. He had to admire that.

Further, he was having a hard time keeping his hands off her. That was the last thing she needed. For that matter, it was the last thing he needed, too.

He couldn't afford to let passion cloud the issue. Until he felt whole again, he wasn't fit company for man nor beast. And certainly not a fit companion for a wonderful woman like Emily.

Maybe he should say all those things to her, but why give her false hope? Why have her waiting for something that might never happen?

"Are you saying you want me to leave? Is that what you're telling me, Jake?"

"Stay as long as you like, Emily, but please don't expect anything of me. I have nothing left to give."

Her heart was in her eyes when she looked at him. He almost caved in and went to her. He almost begged her to stay.

"Take care, Jake," she finally said, then she picked up her purse and walked out the door.

He could hear her car starting up in the driveway. Jake shoved himself off the cabinet and bolted for the front door.

"Em?" he called. *"Emily!"*

But she had already gone. He went back in to the house and closed the door. If he had been in Mexico, he'd have gotten drunk on tequila.

Emily didn't stop driving until she'd reached her cabin in the woods. Empty silence echoed through her house. There was no little skunk to greet her. She didn't even have any animals in the holding area for rehabilitation.

Without unpacking her bag, she changed clothes, then tromped through the woods looking for an animal to rescue. Not that she wanted one to be hurt or caught in a trap. Quite the contrary, she was always delighted when her searches yielded nothing.

She just needed something to do, that was all. She needed something to occupy her mind.

When she reached the stream where Gwendolyn had left her, Emily sat down and waited, very still. Once she thought she caught a glimpse of two black-and-white tails, but then she saw it was only a bush blowing in the breeze.

It was going to rain. Good. At least the long drought would finally end.

Emily sat in the woods until the first drops began to fall. Then she went back into the house, shut the door, closed the blinds, called her mom, turned the phone ringer off and went to bed.

She wished she could sleep until it was all over. Whatever *it* was.

Jake didn't go to Mexico and get drunk on tequila. He flew to Alaska and climbed Mount McKinley. Solo.

He'd climbed McKinley many times, but standing on the summit of South Peak never failed to stir him. It was called the top of the continent for a good reason. Not only was it the highest point in North America, but it offered a sweeping vista of the surrounding national park that took his breath away.

With his face to the east he took a silver-framed photograph sealed in a plastic bag out of his pocket and placed it on a small outcropping of rock. His trusted right-hand man smiled back at him.

"Jamal, this one's for you."

Jake knelt in the ice and snow and said a prayer for his friend, then began his descent down the mountain.

A golden eagle soared over him, and on the lower slopes moose and caribou lifted their massive heads to see who was invading their terrain.

"It's all right, big guys. We're here for the same reason," Jake said, and suddenly he knew it was true. Just as the mountains sustained the wildlife, they sustained him.

When he reached the base he turned and saluted the mighty giant of Denali, then turned his face south toward home.

Chapter Thirty-Eight

The day Gwendolyn came to visit was the day Jake came home. That was the way Emily would always remember it.

She was on her knees pulling weeds out of the wildflower bed she'd cultivated in front of her cabin when Gwendolyn poked her nose under her arm.

"Well, hello, sweetcakes." Emily rubbed her head, then her tummy. "Getting fat, aren't you." There was a stirring in the bushes, and she glanced over her shoulder to find Gwendolyn's companion hiding there, peering out with his beady little black eyes.

That was when the truth hit Emily.

"You're pregnant! Why, you sassy little old thing."

Suddenly she had tears in her eyes. There was a big empty spot in the pit of her stomach that was going to swallow her up if she didn't do something.

She stood up and dusted off the seat of her pants. "You

newlyweds wait right there. I'll go in the house and get
you a treat.''

When she came back outside the skunks were gone, and
there stood Jake.

''Hello, Emily.''

''Oh.'' She put her hand over her heart. It was beating
so hard she thought it might fly right out of her chest. ''I
didn't hear you drive up.''

''Maybe I should have called first.''

''No…no, that's all right.'' What to do? What to say?
They hadn't parted under the best of circumstances. She
hadn't said, ''Don't come to me unless you mean it.'' Why
hadn't she said that? Was that why he had come? To get
back together with her?

Or maybe he'd come merely to say hello. Or goodbye.
A true and lasting goodbye.

She didn't think she could endure that. These past few
lonely days, she hadn't had Jake, but at least she'd had
hope.

Suddenly she sank onto the front-porch steps.

''Em? Are you all right?''

Jake started toward her, and Emily held up her hand to
stop him.

''Don't come any closer—unless you mean to stay.'' He
looked startled, and Emily pushed her hair back from her
hot face. ''I really mean that, Jake. I'm through being Miss
Goody Two-shoes.''

Jake's mouth curved upward. ''Miss Goody Two-
shoes?''

Emily wasn't going to be won over by a smile. Nossiree,
Bob. She was playing for keeps. All or nothing at all.

''I'm not a fair-weather kind of woman, and I don't want
a fair-weather kind of man. I'm in this with you for the
long haul, and unless that's the way you feel about me, too,

then I want you to get in your car and leave and never come back.''

Jake stood in her yard looking at her for a long, long time. Then he did something that astonished Emily, and delighted her so much she knew she'd love this man as long as she lived.

He knelt in front of her, unmindful of the dirt, then took her hand and kissed it and said, ''Miss Emily, I love you more than life itself, and I want to marry you, even if you have changed your name to Miss Goody Two-shoes.''

''Is that proposal real, or are you just trying to get on my good side?''

''It's real.'' He scooped her into his arms and kissed her until they both lost their breaths. ''Can I still get on your good side, too?''

''Definitely.''

''You'll have to show me which one it is. I forget.''

''We'll have to remedy that.''

She took his hand, started inside, and he said, ''You didn't give me an answer, Emily.''

''I will.''

''When?''

''Soon.''

He kissed her again, and the passion between them was so strong it would not be denied. They left a trail of clothes from the doorway to the bed. Her kicked-off shorts, his crumpled-up jeans, her blouse with the top button gone where she'd ripped it away, his shirt jerked over his head and wadded in a ball, their shoes overturned, shoelaces tangled together.

Everything was vivid to her—the blood-red of the upholstered chair contrasting sharply with the gleaming whiteness of her blouse. The rainbow on the wall where the sun caught the colors of the prisms hanging on the lampshade.

The silence of the deep woods that echoed through the cabin. The clean smell of Jake's skin. The hot pleasure that jolted through her when he entered her.

She felt newly born, a Venus rising from the sea with the dark waters still swirling about her feet. With this man there would always be undercurrents of danger, days of uncertainty while he challenged the mountains, weeks of waiting alone in an empty house, an empty bed.

And yet...

He was magic. He was her hero. He was her world.

Without him she was nothing more than a sleepwalker, fumbling her way through the dark. To live that way was unthinkable to Emily, and she knew what her answer would be.

She embraced him, took him deep inside and welcomed him home.

With his face only inches from hers, he said, "I love you, Em. I've always loved you and I always will."

She knew he spoke the truth. In her bones, she knew.

"I love you, too, Jake."

She wrapped her arms and legs around him and fell slowly into the magic that can only happen in the presence of true love.

Chapter Thirty-Nine

September 15, 2001

So much has happened in the last few days it's hard to know where to begin.

I'll start with Jake.

He showed up out of the blue, just walked in one day while I was sitting beside Michael's bed and said, "Hello, Anne. I hope you don't mind that I didn't call first, but I have to talk to Michael." I said to him, "Well, of course, I don't mind, I'm happy to see you, Jake."

Actually, I didn't know whether I was happy to see him or not. It all depended on why he had come. I know what happened in Atlanta. At least, I know most of it. And I know that Emily came back with a broken heart.

I also know that she came back with a dogged determination to get on with her life, no matter what, and I applauded that. She's made of stern stuff, my youngest daughter.

Michael would be so proud of her. Well, of course, he is proud of her, because I've told him everything. When he wakes up I don't want him to be confused about his own family. So I keep him abreast of events.

I know he hears. I just know it, but I wish he'd give some sign.

"I could use a sign here, Michael," I told him last night after I'd recounted how I'd advised Emily to be there when Jake got home, and how it had all turned out so badly.

"I could use some reassurance," I said. "Did I tell her the right thing, or am I letting my own romantic nature lead my children astray?"

Nothing. Not a single, solitary movement.

Oh, sometimes I get so discouraged. And yet I know I must not. I know, I know. Life goes on. With or without us.

Anyway, back to Jake... He asked to talk to Michael and I said yes.

Here's how the conversation went from there:

"Why don't you stand on the other side of the bed close enough so he can hear you, Jake?"

When he moved to the side of the bed, I said, "Michael, Jake wants to talk to you. Now you pay attention, darling, because he's come a long way, and from the look on his face, I'd say that what he's going to tell you is very important."

I squeezed Michael's hand, then told Jake I would wait outside in the hall. I don't usually do that. I stay. I don't want anybody saying things that might distress Michael, and I certainly don't want anybody coming in here and acting as if he's nothing more than a piece of furniture, talking over him and about him as if he had no more brain than a turnip.

Of course, I don't have to worry about that with Jake. He's the kind of man you trust instantly. He's the kind of man you look at one time and say to yourself, "My daughter's safe with him."

Yes, I know, I know. But in spite of everything that has happened, I still think that.

Anyhow, Jake said he wanted me to stay, that what he had to say was meant for me, too.

"Michael, it's me, Jake," he said, and when he took my husband's hand, I saw tears in his eyes.

Well, I can't tell you how that made me feel. Proud. Even vindicated. A man who is not afraid to let his emotions show is a real man in my book. A true hero.

"The mountain has been giving me a hard time lately, Michael, and I've been wrestling with the demons I'm sure you conquered years ago. I wish you'd been able to give me some advice. It might have saved us some heartache. Your daughter and me."

Well, when I heard Jake mention Emily, my insides fluttered the way they always do when I'm nervous, and then I looked at his face and everything just settled down. Like a warm blanket being tossed over a bunch of cold, unruly children.

"I thought about giving it all up, then I made myself climb again, and when I reached the peak, the mountain gave me its benediction."

The room got so quiet you could hear a pin drop. You could hear a heart break and then slowly, ever so slowly, piece itself back together.

I was holding Michael's hand on one side and Jake on the other, and I swear to you, Jake's face was glowing as if he were in the presence of God.

Was it the mountain or Michael that inspired such devotion? I like to think it was both. I like to think that even while he's still in a coma, my husband was responsible for teaching Jake how to follow his heart.

My Michael has always done that. Followed his heart. And the reward has been joy, indescribable joy.

Well, Jake cleared his throat, unclogging the tears, I suspect, and then he looked at me in a way that said, "Pay attention now. This is the important part."

"Michael, I'm on my way to see your daughter, and if she lets me through the door, I'm going to ask her to marry me—if that's all right with you."

We both waited, hoping for some sign, hoping that at last we'd told Michael something so important he couldn't stay locked in that deep dark place so far away from the people who love him.

If I let myself, I could imagine a tiny movement of his hand. So slight, so small. Like a baby bird trying to decide whether to get on the edge of the nest and really flex his untried wings.

"Seeing you with Anne showed me what love is. You've set a high standard, Michael, and I intend to follow it."

Wake up, Michael, I wanted to scream. WAKE UP. If you're ever going to come out of that coma, now is the time.

I didn't scream, of course. I read somewhere recently that if you've been very close to a person, you can communicate with them through mental telepathy. No matter where they are. Even in a coma. And so I thought it with my whole might.

"Well," Jake said, "that's about it. I'm going to Emily's cabin now, and if she'll have me, we'll both be back for your blessing."

Jake glanced across at me, so hopeful, so young.

"Don't worry," I said, and then I led him to the door and he hugged me and I cried a little, and he hugged me again.

Oh, he's going to be a wonderful son-in-law. Daniel is going to be tickled pink, and Hannah...well, Hannah will just have to get over it, that's all.

She'll come through for her sister. Family loyalty is important to her. As it is to all our children. Michael and I can be proud of that.

The sun's going down now and soon it will be dark in this room. I'm glad. With my eyes closed and a cocoon of blackness around me, I feel something Michael must be feeling. A sort of safety. A sense of peace.

I have breathing room. That's it. Time and space in which to take stock, to reconsider my life. I think such things as, if I had it to do all over again, would I give up my career as a pianist? That's an easy yes. How about this one—would I have learned to climb so I could have spent more time with Michael? I don't know. After all these years, I still don't know.

Maybe if I'd been on Everest the day of the avalanche, Michael would have been safe inside his tent like the rest of the crew. If I'd been there, he would be in my bed at Belle Rose right now, reaching for me with that certain gleam in his eye.

I can't flay myself that way. I won't.

What is Michael thinking in his soft cocoon of darkness? Is he reconsidering the choices he's made in his life? Is he thinking about his children? About me?

Or is he merely drifting, floating above us all, disconnected? A wanderer who can't get home again, who can't even remember what home is like?

Oh, it can't be. I won't let it happen that way.

In a little while the night nurse will be in here to check Michael's vital signs. She'll ask if there's anything she can get for me. A cup of juice? An extra blanket? And I'll say no, I have everything I need.

Then I'll put on my gown—the blue one that's gone soft with so many washings, the one Michael likes so much—and I'll climb in bed beside my husband and wrap my arms around him and say, "Don't you dare leave me, Michael Westmoreland. I would die without you. I'm not going to let you leave. Do you hear me?"

Chapter Forty

I hear you, Anne. I feel you pressed against me, smell your hair, feel the softness of your gown. Is it the blue one?

I'm trying to come back to you, but I can't seem to reach you. There's so much fog...I've lost my way.

I feel something damp against my skin. Are you crying, Anne? Don't cry, my love. Don't cry. I'm not going to leave you. I'll always be with you.

Always.

* * * * *

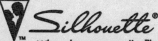

Welcome to

 **Silhouette**

DREAMSCAPES...

a world where passion and danger mingle together...and the temptation of dark, sensual romance awaits.

In December 2001, look for these four alluring romances:

FROM A DISTANCE
by Emilie Richards

THE PERFECT KISS
by Amanda Stevens

SEA GATE
by Maura Seger

SOMETHING BEAUTIFUL
by Marilyn Tracy

*Available at
your favorite retail outlet.*

 **Silhouette®**

Where love comes alive™

INTIMATE MOMENTS™
is proud to present

Romancing the Crown

With the help of their powerful allies, the royal family of Montebello is determined to find their missing heir. But the search for the beloved prince is not without danger—or passion!

This exciting twelve book series begins in January and continues throughout the year with these fabulous titles:

Available at your favorite retail outlet.

Silhouette®
Where love comes alive™

Visit Silhouette at www.eHarlequin.com

SIMRC

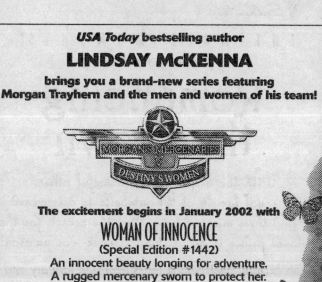